YOUNG TOM

AUTHOR'S NOTE

Chronologically the stories dealing with Tom Barber run in the following sequence—*Young Tom*, *The Retreat*, *Uncle Stephen*—though actually they were written in the reverse order and each is complete in itself. All the characters except Roger, Pincher, and Barker are imaginary.

F.R.

YOUNG TOM

or

Very Mixed Company

---

by

FORREST REID

What call'st thou solitude? Is not the Earth
With various living creatures, and the Air,
Replenished, and all these at thy command
To come and play before thee? Knowest thou not
Their language and their ways? . . . With these
Find pastime.

Paradise Lost

First published in 1944 by Faber and Faber
This edition and introduction published in February 1987 by
GMP Publishers Ltd, P O Box 247, London N15 6RW, England.

Distributed in the USA by
Subterranean Company
P O Box 10233
Eugene
Oregon 97440

British Library Cataloguing in Publication Data

Reid, Forrest
Young Tom.
I. Title
823'.912 [F] PR6035.E43

ISBN 0-85449-055-8

Printed and bound by the Guernsey Press, Guernsey, C.I.

INTRODUCTION

At any given time there are a number of writers whose reputations languish, awaiting critical rediscovery. Often, as was the case with Barbara Pym, a loyal readership maintains some level of popularity for the works, and particular favourites find their champions, until word slowly spreads or fame suddenly alights upon the neglected name.

Forrest Reid (1875–1947) was very highly regarded in his lifetime, and writers as different as Walter de la Mare and E.M. Forster recognised the lasting qualities of his fiction, from *The Kingdom of Twilight* (1904) to his masterpiece *Young Tom*, which won the James Tait Black Memorial Prize for the best novel of 1944.

Reid's novels of innocence, experience, and the deep longing for companionship are ripe for rediscovery. They have never lacked their supporters, and for those who read them in childhood they hold a special place in the heart. Their subject is almost always childhood, and that special loneliness of the sensitive child, whose longing for an ideal companion takes him into realms of fantasy and dream. It is the realistic world of these dreams that is Forrest Reid's unique preserve: he creates a complete and immediately recognisable world that is quite different from the fictional world of, say, L.P. Hartley, whose work is in many ways similar.

Francis King, comparing Reid to Forster, wrote, "If one sets a descriptive passage by Reid against one by Forster it is nearly always Reid—so lucid, so limpid, so totally without affection—who comes out the better." This unaffected, clear-sighted identification with the emotions and aspirations of childhood and adolescence is Forrest Reid's contribution to the literature of childhood. But he has been criticised, by Peter Coveney for example, as having an "idealising dishonesty" about his work, and accusations of escapism and over-sentimentalisation have also been made against him. Reid himself was the first to acknowledge that he "preferred the literature of escape, and what *I* should call the literature of imagination, for the escape is only from the impermanent into the permanent."

E.M. Forster, who was to write the introduction to the single volume edition of the Tom Barber trilogy, of which *Young Tom* was the last to be written, had said of Reid's work as early as 1919: "When his genius gains the recognition that has so strangely been withheld from it, he will be ranked with the artists who have preferred to see life steadily than to see it whole and who have concentrated their regard upon a single point, a point which, when rightly focussed, may perhaps make all the surrounding landscape intelligible." Reid's landscape is a landscape of familiar loss, a world of recent gardens and idyllic summers, a world where the pain of the real world is, however, not denied, as it would be in the work of J.M. Barrie, nor trivialised, as in the work of Hugh Lofting. Reid was a great admirer of Lofting's Doctor Dolittle novels, bracketing them with the work of E. Nesbit in terms of quality and attractiveness. He wrote of them that they "are not fairy-stories, they are not adventure-stories, they are not matter-of-fact stories, they are not animal stories (at least of any hitherto known type), but are a blend of all four." It is similarly difficult to classify Reid's own stories. To stress the fact that young Tom Barber can speak to animals, and they to him, would be to emphasise an aspect of the story-telling which is utterly convincing in its penetration of the child's thought-processes. But to ignore this essential childish make-believe would be to deny the novel its *raison d'être*.

Young Tom is the third of the Tom Barber trilogy, which began with *Uncle Stephen* in 1931, was continued with *The Retreat* in 1936, and was only concluded some eight years after that. The three novels form a backward progress from adolescence to childhood: in *Uncle Stephen* Tom is on the threshold of manhood, in *The Retreat* he is 13, at the beginning of his adolescence, and in *Young Tom* he is 11. Reid, then, was almost seventy when he concluded the work he had been thinking about since 1914, a kind of *Bildungsroman* in reverse. Reid wrote to a friend, "I suppose you may regard this as a sign of my own gradual—or rapid—approach to second childhood", wondering "if books were ever written backwards before."

Yet the trilogy reads as naturally and truly as if it were recently lived experience. It has none of the knowingness of Laurie Lee's *Cider with Rosie*, none of the sense of encroaching menace we find in Elizabeth Bowen's evocations of lost golden summers in Ireland. The absence of adult intrusion into the narrative sensibility focuses the reader's attention and sympathy entirely on the central character—we believe, with him, in the characters who people his world. These may be real (his family, his enemy Max Sabine, his companion Pascoe, the handsome farm-boy James-Arthur), or animals (Roger, Pincher, Barker, the dogs—described in the Author's Note as not imaginary characters—and, very importantly, Edward, the squirrel), or even ghostly (the figure of Ralph). The dividing line between real and imaginary is always vague in Tom's mind—and so it must be for the reader too. The turning-point of the novel, Max's killing of Edward, should be as shocking and upsetting to the reader as it was to Tom. His desire for revenge, and his carrying out of his plan of revenge are not mere childish over-reaction. They are acute reflections of innocence consciously reacting to the ravages of experience.

The reader is not, however, asked to judge Tom sentimentally. Max, unsympathetic to Tom from the start, is not portrayed as a villain, but just as a boy. His violence is as unmotivated and inexplicable as children's violence often is. It is not to be read as a symbol, but is to be accepted as a fact of life. Tom's interest in "curiosities of natural history" might be seen to be misdirected—human curiosities tend to be outside of his interest, and experience teaches him (if it teaches him anything) that these are as much a part of the living world as the animals with whom he finds it easier to establish a meaningful relationship.

The life of the mind of young Tom, rather than the life of young Tom, is the subject-matter of the trilogy. It is a mind that is endlessly attracted to the natural world, to myth, and to beauty. There is a kind of gentle pantheistic paganism, a tendency, particularly in the older Tom, towards a Greek philosophical ideal. This is not an affectation of pre-lapsarian *angst*—quite the reverse. Reid himself had been at Cambridge with Ronald Firbank and described that writer's work as "decadent . . . hovering between Wilde and Norman Douglas." There is nothing decadent in Reid, although his search for ideal companionship, and his celebration of masculine beauty have given rise to various levels of phychological speculation.

In *Young Tom* when Tom sees the sixteen-year-old farm boy James-Arthur naked, what is stressed is the natural innocence of the scene—only with the hindsight of adult experience does the situation become questionable:

> . . . in Tom's eyes he somehow did not look naked. He had simply emerged from his soiled and much-patched clothing like a butterfly from a chrysalis, and the contrast between his fair hair and the golden brown of his body and limbs appeared to the smaller boy as attractive as anything could be. In fact James-Arthur, merely by divesting himself of his clothes, had instantly become part of the natural scene, like the grass and the trees and the river and the sky, and the dragon-fly asleep upon his water-lily.

This is highly characteristic of Reid, with its insistence on nature and naturalness, and with that level of personalisation that "his water-lily" reveals. The reader should see nature as Tom does, and should judge as Tom does, a little later, "it couldn't be disgusting, however, unless there was someone there to be disgusted, and at present there was no one."

Of course, nascent sexuality is important in *Young Tom*, and the final pages give a brilliant dream image that is imbued with just the kind of ambiguity the young adolescent feels in the face of growing awareness of sexuality. Reid, however, chooses to keep the expression of sexuality repressed in all his works. *Brian Westby*, his most realistic and most adult-centred novel, is a classic of unstated affection between an older and a younger man. This very lack of affirmation, notably in *Uncle Stephen*, lends an air of mystery to Tom's discoveries, and it is this mystery which gives the reader the pleasure of sharing the secrets, the uncertainties. the boy's eye view of the world. Adult knowingness would destroy that world and that pleasure.

The world of Forrest Reid resembles a lost world in more ways than one. An Ulsterman, described by one critic as "the first Ulster writer of European status", his Ireland is a relatively untroubled land. Tom Barber is the child of a well-established middle-class family—tramps, the unemployed, and farm-boys know their station, although the figure of the tramp in *Young Tom* is nicely subversive. Tom's world is not very far removed from the real world; he is emerging from his cocoon at his own pace, and treasuring every positive moment as he does so.

Edwin Muir described the world of Reid's novels as lying "outside time and society". This is what gives the stories their lasting appeal. It is a commonplace to speak of the past as another country, but Forrest Reid helps us relive that past in an everlasting present. In evoking the minutely observed childhood of Tom Barber he takes us all back to memories, true or false, idealised or romanticised, of our own earliest years. But that difficult passage, where experience breaks in on innocence, where the child is torn between the wish for adult knowledge and the need to cling to childhood security (so often the subject of the *Bidungsroman* from Dickens to Lawrence and beyond) is handled with a complete lack of sentimentality, regret, or nostalgia.

It is not a lost world, and it is not a world of eternal childhood. "Beautiful boys in beautiful landscapes" it may be. But there is an underlying ethos to the novels which gives a resonance to Tom's search for the perfect companion and the perfect day's enjoyment with that companion. The novels are an expression of the search for what can give a meaning to life. And, simplistic though that may seem, the search is an agonising and complex one. The seventy-year-old writer was still engaged upon that search, and in the Tom Barber trilogy traced the search back almost to its very beginnings. The values of the novels are, indeed, simple values—companionship, nature, philosophy, and a realistic acceptance of the surrounding world. Tom tries, in his way, to shape the world according to his desires. But the world will not be shaped: the Max Sabines of the world are always with us, and no amount of running away to Granny's can alter that.

Forrest Reid's writing was all a kind of search for the childhood ideal of the lost garden, a search which he himself described, in his "spiritual autobiography" *Apostate* (1927), as "a kind of crying for Elysium." He treads a very thin line between the sublimated and the sublime, between the scrupulously realistic and the "dreamy contemplation of a world shifting uncertainly between recollection and imagination" (to quote from the final transcendent moments of *Young Tom*). And the world he presents is totally convincing, an entire world, at the same time personal and universal.

For Reid this was the function of art, to explore and express "that divine homesickness, that . . . longing for an Eden from which each one of us is exiled." In taking us back to such a world he fulfils Forster's dictum of making "all the surrounding landscape intelligible." A world no longer innocent needs constantly to be reminded of the potential and remembered innocence that is necessary to humanity. It is, as Reid wrote in *Apostate*, "a country whose image was stamped upon our soul before we opened our eyes on earth, and all our life is little more than a trying to get back there, our art a mapping of its mountains and streams."

The greatness of the Tom Barber trilogy is that it takes the reader on a voyage of discovery of that uncharted, but strangely familiar country: its loss a necessary part of life—its rediscovery one of life's unexpected joys.

John McRae

Part One
THE FRIENDS

CHAPTER I

"Take your hands out of your pockets and don't stand there dreaming," had been Daddy's farewell words. Spoken in a distinctly impatient voice too, so that Tom, while he waved goodbye and watched the car receding down the drive, felt both surprised and annoyed. Yet these same words when pronounced by Mother (as they usually were about fifty times a day), never annoyed him in the least. Coming from Daddy—who didn't even practise what he preached—and above all coming in that irritable tone, they were quite another thing; therefore, having withdrawn his hands in token of obedience, Tom felt justified, immediately afterwards, in putting them back again. True, this gesture of independence was largely directed at William, whose self-righteous and reproving gaze he perceived to be fixed upon him. William said nothing, but he shook his head pessimistically before proceeding with his work. William was clipping edges—and no doubt clipping them very neatly—yet Tom didn't see why that need make him look so dourly conscious of possessing every virtue—all the less attractive ones at any rate. He ought to have looked like Adam (see *Paradise Lost*—Mother's recollected version of it), and he didn't. In fact, Tom could imagine some thoughtless young green shoot, filled with an ardent zest of life, wriggling excitedly up through the brown soil, catching one glimpse of William's sour countenance, and hastily retreating underground again.

The strange thing was that nothing of the kind happened. If anywhere, it was in Tom's own private garden that plants exhibited signs of nervousness. The struggle for life there was bitter in the extreme, and not a few had given it up as hopeless, while the survivors hung limp and melancholy heads. Turning to this questionable oasis now, he could not help feeling that last night's attentions had only increased its resemblance to a violated grave, and he stooped to pull out a weed, and to press down the earth round a recently transplanted orange lily. The officious William was watching him, of course, and very soon came his grumpy counsel: "You let them alone, Master Tom, and don't be always worretin' and pokin' at them. Plants is like men; they can't abide naggin' and fussin'. . . . When I was a wee lad, no bigger'n what you are now, I'd have had that patch lovely."

"So *you* say!" Tom retorted, though a sense of justice presently compelled him to add; "Well, maybe you would."

For though William might be a cantankerous, disagreeable old man, for ever grousing and complaining, all his surroundings—flowers, shrubs, paths, and lawn—were undeniable and brilliant testimonials to his efficiency. On this morning of the last day of June the garden was looking its very best—a wonderful blaze of colour—and deliberately Tom inhaled its fragrance—the varied scents of stocks, roses, mignonette, and sweet-briar—all mixed together in one aromatic medley.

It was going to be very hot later, he thought; for even now, early as it was, he could feel the sun pleasantly warm on his bare head and neck and hands, and penetrating through his grey flannel jacket and tennis shirt. Two young thrushes were swinging up and down on a slender prunus branch as if it were a seesaw. He tried to draw William's attention to them, but William, continuing his slow methodical progress with the edge-clippers, would not even look, merely grunted. That was because he thought birds received a great deal too much encouragement in this garden: if he had had his way he would have shot them, like Max Sabine, or else covered up everything eatable with nets.

The abundance of birds was partly due to the glen beside the house, and partly to the fact that Daddy took an interest in them, hung up coconuts for them, supplied them with baths, and fed them all through the winter. Tom liked birds too, but he very much preferred animals. Doctor Macrory, to be sure, had told him he would like penguins, because penguins were much the same as dogs, came when you called them, and allowed you to pat them on their broad solid backs—good substantial thumps, which they accepted in the proper spirit. But he had never seen a penguin, except a stuffed one in Queen's University Museum, and even Doctor Macrory thought they might be troublesome to keep as pets unless you happened to be a fishmonger. . . .

Suddenly there was a tapping on the window behind him, which he knew, without turning round, to be a signal from Mother. The signal was to remind him that he was supposed to be on his way to the Rectory, where he did lessons with Althea Sabine, under the supervision of Miss Sabine, who was Althea's Aunt Rachel, and the Rector's sister.

But there was no hurry; in fact he didn't know why Miss Sabine wanted him at the Rectory at all this morning, for she had set them no lessons. This meant that the long summer holidays had already begun; and whatever she had to say to him she might just as well have said yesterday. Anyhow, it would be for the last time; since he was going to school after the summer.

That had been decided at Miss Sabine's own suggestion. She had called specially to talk the matter over with Daddy and Mother, and apparently her report had pleased them, though what she had actually said he did not know, except that she regarded him as "quite a talented little boy". He would not have known even this had not Mother let it out inadvertently, for to himself Miss Sabine had always expressed her approval in a very brief and dry fashion. Yet somehow he liked her dryness, and liked doing lessons with her; and though she had never told him so, and never showed it openly, he knew she knew this and that it pleased her.

Miss Sabine kept house for her brother, there being no Mrs. Sabine. Poor Mrs. Sabine, indeed, was so much a thing of the past that Althea had once told him her mother had died before she was born. Tom had puzzled over this, having heard of a similar phenomenon in the case of a sheep who had been struck by lightning. But Althea had not mentioned a thunder-storm, and delicacy had prevented him from doing so either. Mother, when he repeated the story at home, declared it was all nonsense. . . .

A second and more imperative tap on the window at this point interrupted his meditations; so he left William and the thrushes, and proceeded on down the short drive as far as the gate, where he found Doctor Macrory's Barker waiting for him.

The gate was shut, but Roger or Pincher would easily have found a way in; it was just like lazy old Barker not to bother. "Take your hands out of your pockets and don't stand there dreaming!" Tom told him sharply, but Barker only wagged a stumpy tail.

It was largely his fashion of mooching along, never in a hurry, never excited, never demonstrative beyond a tail-wag—which he made as brief as possible—that gave Barker his sluggish and slouchy appearance. He was the most phlegmatic and independent dog Tom had ever met. Of course, he was old—older even than Roger, the collie from Denny's farm, though he too was well on the other side of middle-age—and much older than Pincher, the Sabines' rough-haired fox-terrier. Indeed, he was old enough to be Pincher's great-grandfather, Tom supposed. All three were his friends, and spent a considerable portion of their time with him. It was their sole point of union, however, for they never dreamed of associating together in his absence. Meeting them occasionally on his daily rounds, Doctor Macrory would stop to discuss the "Dogs' Club", as he called it, and question Tom as to their several breeds—a joke which had begun to pall slightly, though it was still received with invariable politeness. They might not be show dogs, Tom thought, but he couldn't see why it should be less aristocratic to be descended from a lot of ancient families than from only one. This view Doctor Macrory himself admitted to be reasonable. And after all, it was his own dog Barker who required most explanation, though you could easily see he was an Old-English sheepdog from his face, his big clumsy paws, and his rough woolly coat of several shades of grey, both in colour and texture remarkably like the hearthrug Mother had made last winter for the study. The three were as different in temperament as they were in their coats. Pincher was restless, for ever getting into scrapes, excitable, and possessed of a sort of primitive, errand-boy sense of humour, vulgar and extremely knowing. Roger was emotional and demonstrative; swift, graceful, lithe; with a tail like a waving ostrich plume. Roger was Tom's darling, and they could sit side by side for a long time with their arms round each other, immersed in a warm bath of affection, while Barker regarded their sloppiness with indifference, and Pincher with impatience. . . .

All the same, it was Barker who was at the gate now, and he wanted Tom to come down to the river. He nearly always did, for that matter, however busy you might be with more important things. "Can't you see I'm going to the Rectory?" Tom asked him; and Barker looked disappointed.

This, Tom felt, was understandable, for it was just the right kind of morning for the river, and certainly not one to be wasted indoors. The myriad voices of Nature were calling—whispering in the trees that overhung and cast deep pools of shadow on the sunlit road—calling more loudly and imperatively from bird and beast and insect. Everywhere was life and the eager joy of life. The very air seemed alive, and from the earth a living strength was pushing upwards and outwards—visible in each separate blade of grass and delicate meadow flower no less than in the great chestnut-tree standing at the corner where the road turned.

From the tangled hawthorn hedge, though its bloom had fallen, came a fresh, cool, green smell. Unfortunately Tom and Barker, tramping along the dusty highway, were on the wrong side of it. On the other side, as they both knew, far more was happening. On the other side was a ditch, where, in a jungle of nettles, vetches, and wild parsnips, young thrushes and blackbirds and sparrows would be hiding. A rook flying out of the chestnut-tree cawed a greeting as he passed over their heads. Two white cabbage butterflies, circling about each other in their strange fashion, flitted across the road and were lost to sight. Barker, pausing by a stile, again mentioned the river.

"No," said Tom emphatically; and after a moment, as a somewhat feeble consolation: "Anyhow, what would we do?"

"Fish for stones," Barker replied promptly.

But Tom had guessed he would say this, and remained unmoved. "Yes, *you'd* fish for them, and I'd sit on the bank and get splashed all over with mud and water."

Barker said no more, not really being importunate. It was strange, all the same, that this fishing for stones should so appeal to him. It had no charm for the other dogs; they never even attempted it; yet Barker could spend happy hours merely dragging stone after stone from the river bed, and dropping each one carefully beside Tom for the latter to arrange in a heap. It was a dirty job, too, because the river bed was soft, and Barker would emerge from it, a large stone in his mouth, and his face so plastered with mud as to be unrecognizable. He must at the same time have swallowed quantities, besides getting it into his eyes and nostrils; yet this did not seem to trouble him, and he would go on as long as Tom's patience lasted. What the latter couldn't understand was why he should have to be present at all. There was nothing to hinder Barker now, for instance, from going down to the river by himself, and spending the rest of the morning fishing for stones; yet Tom knew he wouldn't; and he was right; Barker accompanied him as far as the Rectory gate, and then turned and trotted off at his customary pace, unvarying as the wheels of a clock. But he went in the direction of his own home, not of the river.

CHAPTER II

The Rectory hall door was open when Tom reached it, so he walked straight on in without ringing the bell. In the dining-room, where they did lessons, he found both Miss Sabine and Althea seated at the table, snipping off the tops and tails of gooseberries. Mother thought there must be foreign, probably Spanish, blood in the Sabines, which was what made them all so vivid-looking. At breakfast this morning she had said so, and also that there was something masculine about Miss Sabine's whole style and appearance, due partly, perhaps, to the way she dressed. Tom, however, could see nothing masculine about her, unless it was that Miss Sabine looked big and strong and had a tiny black moustache. In every way she suggested strength—strength of character, strength of mind, strength of purpose. Her skin was almost swarthy, her hair jet black, and when she was really angry, as he had seen her on one memorable occasion with Max, her eyes literally flashed.

"Good morning, Tom," she now greeted him, in her firm deep voice; while Althea said "Hello!" and giggled.

Tom returned Miss Sabine's "good morning", but took no notice of Althea, whose habit of giggling at nothing displeased him. Althea, at any rate, was vivid enough, with cheeks like apples, and her hair hanging down in sleek black pigtails. At the moment, however, he was much less interested either in her, or in Mother's discoveries, than in a row of brand-new books, with brilliant bindings and gilt edges, spread out in the middle of the table. Having cast a rapid glance at these, he determinedly looked away, and coloured when he saw Althea watching him with a kind of sly amusement. It was very like her, he thought: she was always amused when you found yourself in some delicate situation and didn't quite know what to do. Not that she was a bad kid on the whole. There was at least nothing mean or treacherous about her, as there was about Max. . . .

"I expect you've been wondering, Tom, why I asked you to come back this morning," Miss Sabine said. "It was simply because those books didn't arrive till after you had gone yesterday, though the man in the shop promised faithfully to send them out in plenty of time. I want you to choose one as a small memento; or perhaps I should say a prize, for of course it is really that."

Tom's blush deepened, and Althea began to hum a little tune, so that he could have kicked her. Nevertheless he managed to jerk out: "Thanks awfully, Miss Sabine."

"Well, you'd better have a look at them," Miss Sabine observed, since his shyness seemed to have reduced him to immobility. "You mayn't like *any* of them, for I could only guess; so if there's some other book you'd prefer instead, I hope you'll tell me."

After this she tactfully resumed her gooseberry-snipping, nor did she once glance at him while he was making his choice.

The first book he took up was Macaulay's *Lays of Ancient Rome*, the only volume he had already rejected in his mind. But Althea, who had *no* tact, was still covertly watching him, and he turned his back upon her.

There were more than a dozen books to choose from, and Miss Sabine must have gone to some trouble in selecting them. Here were *The Talisman* and *David Copperfield*; *Huckleberry Finn*, and *The Golden Treasury* bound in leather; *Tom Brown's Schooldays*, *Westward Ho!*, *Grimm's' Fairy Tales*, *King Solomon's Mines*, and *Treasure Island*. Each attracted him; but he already possessed a tattered copy of *Grimm*, and the attraction of *The Talisman* and *Westward Ho!* was somewhat faint. *The Golden Treasury*, moreover, was poetry, though if it had been Edgar Allan Poe's poetry he might have taken it. As it was, he lifted each book in turn, glanced through it, and looked at the pictures if there were any. But this was an act of politeness pure and simple, for very quickly he had made up his mind that the choice lay between two books only—*Nat the Naturalist*, by George Manville Fenn, and *Curiosities of Natural History*, by Frank Buckland. He would have decided on the latter at once had it not been in four volumes—First Series, Second Series, Third Series, and Fourth Series—therefore it might seem greedy to choose it when all the others were in one volume only. True, the *Curiosities* volumes were less sumptuously bound, and had neither gilt nor olivine edges. If you took them individually, they looked less expensive than the others, and it suddenly occurred to him that very likely they *were* to be regarded as separate books, so he lifted the first and said: "I'd like this, please."

"Well, I think you've made an excellent choice," Miss Sabine agreed, "though I haven't read it myself, and picked it out just because I thought from the title it might interest you."

"But—but——" Tom stammered, for Miss Sabine had drawn

all four volumes towards her and was now preparing to write his name in them. Pen in hand she paused, glancing up at him.

"I meant—I thought—there'd be only one," Tom mumbled in confusion.

Miss Sabine smiled: she understood perfectly. "Oh, that's all right," she assured him, looking at him very kindly, and dipping her pen. "They go together: they *are* only one." And she began her inscription, quite a lengthy one, or so it seemed to Tom, for her writing was very large and black, and sprawled over the whole yellowish end-paper.

"And now," she said, pressing down the blotting-paper, "there you are. You certainly deserve all four, and if you do as well at school as you have always done with me, I don't think they'll be the last prizes you'll get."

Tom thanked her once again, beaming all over with a pleasure that lit up like sunshine his plain, freckled, blunt-featured face, and greenish-grey eyes. At the same time he wondered what Althea had got, but did not like to ask since the others had not mentioned it.

Nor, though she accompanied him as far as the garden gate, did Althea mention it when they were alone. "Max is going to camp," was all she told him. "He didn't want to, but his form master or somebody wrote to Dad about it, so he won't be coming home just yet." Then, as Tom received this information in silence: "I suppose you're not interested. . . . I forgot. . . . You don't like him much, do you?"

"No," Tom said.

The remarkable frankness of his agreement did not appear to trouble Althea. "Why?" she asked, without the slightest hint of resentment.

"Because I don't," Tom answered.

Althea was silent for a minute or two, as if mentally turning over this response. He could see, nevertheless, that what she was really searching for was an excuse for pursuing the subject. "I don't think you ought to dislike him," was the very feeble one she eventually found. "I mean—to keep it up in that way. It's wicked."

In spite of his annoyance, Tom laughed. "Do you think he likes *me*?" he said.

"I don't know. I never asked him. But that shouldn't prevent you from setting a good example."

"Yes . . . ?" He looked at her closely. "Why are you sticking on all this? You don't go in much yourself for setting good examples."

"I can't: I've nobody to set them to," Althea sighed. But curiosity once more prevailed, and she said: "I suppose it has something to do with the Fallon boy—James-Arthur."

Tom flushed hotly. "You can suppose what you like," he retorted, and would have left her abruptly had she not caught him by his jacket.

"Don't be so huffy! I only said I *supposed* it was that. And if you want to know why, it was because I heard Max talking to Dad about it, and telling him you oughtn't to be allowed to be friends with a farm boy. . . . So you needn't get in a temper as if it was *my* fault. . . . Aunt Rachel heard him too, and ticked him off for being such a snob."

But Tom by this time had shaken himself free, and with a brief "Good-bye," he made his escape, leaving Althea standing at the gate gazing after him.

CHAPTER III

With the four precious red volumes under his arm he hurried down the road, eager to display them at home. But when he reached the church, a squat little grey stone building with a square tower, he paused. The door was wide open, and he remembered he had never been inside on a weekday, when it must be more interesting, or at any rate different. On Sundays he had to sit in a pew from which he could see little except the upper parts of the congregation, and the whole of Mr. Sabine in his white surplice. Even the stained-glass window was at the opposite side from where he and Daddy and Mother sat, so that he had never been able to examine it closely. This was his chance, for though somebody of course must be inside, it would only be Mrs. Fallon, James-Arthur's mother.

He swung himself over the low, moss-lined wall, and crossed the grass between green graves and dark cypress-trees. Sure enough, Mrs. Fallon emerged at that very moment, carrying a bucket of slops, which she emptied on to the grass. She was obviously not expecting visitors, for her petticoats were extremely tucked up, revealing quite a lot of grey woollen stocking above two stout black boots, large enough to have been James-Arthur's own. Also her head was tied up, like a dumpling, in a blue duster with white spots.

"Good morning, Mrs. Fallon," Tom said, approaching her from behind, so that Mrs. Fallon, who had neither heard nor seen him, jumped.

"Good gracious, Master Tom! You give me quite a turn!"

"Sorry," he apologized. "I didn't mean to. May I go in to the church, Mrs. Fallon—just for a few minutes—unless you've finished and want to lock up?"

But Mrs. Fallon hadn't finished. "You're welcome, dear," she told him, "and if it's the tower, the door's not locked, you've only to push it."

Tom thanked her. "It was really the window I was thinking of," he explained, "but I'd like to go up the tower too."

"You'll not be fiddling with the bell-rope, then, will you, like a good boy?"

He promised, and went in, followed by Mrs. Fallon, who had refilled her bucket from a tap beside the porch.

He went straight to the stained-glass window, through which the sun was pouring, casting warm splashes of coloured light on the whitewashed pillars and on the floor and opposite wall. The window showed an old man wading across a river, carrying a small boy on his shoulders. The man, with his white beard and his staff, Tom knew to be Saint Christopher, and the small boy to be Christ. He also knew that Christ was growing heavier and heavier all the time, though of course the artist could not show this in his picture.

He admired the window for several minutes, trying to remember how the story had ended: then he drew closer that he might read the tablet below, which said that it had been put up by loving grandparents in memory of their grandson, Ralph Seaford, who had died at the age of ten years, and was buried with his parents and infant sister in the churchyard outside.

"It's all very sad, isn't it?" Mrs. Fallon called out cheerfully from the chancel steps, where she was on her knees scrubbing them. But it did not sadden Tom; he only wondered if Ralph Seaford had been fond of the story of Saint Christopher; which in turn led him to wonder what kind of boy he had been. At any rate the old people must have thought a lot of him. . . .

Speculating as to whether Granny in similar circumstances would have put up a window to *him*, he crossed the church, and passing behind the pulpit opened the door leading to the tower. It was not a high tower, and a narrow, winding flight of stone steps soon brought him to a kind of loft, or small square room, in the middle of which the bell-rope hung down stiffly like a giant's pigtail. There were little windows—or rather slits in the wall, for they had no glass—which let in a certain amount of light; and far above, in the dusk beneath the rafters, he could see the bell itself.

The tower and the bell reminded him of a poem which had got Althea into endless trouble while they had been learning it. This was because she could never say "bells, bells, bells, bells, bells, bells, bells," without giggling; and that was only seven times, and once or twice it came oftener. Miss Sabine used to get furious, and Tom, too, had thought Althea very silly: for the repetitions were part of the tune, and the tune was part of the poem. He himself liked it, and had even tried to sing it. Unsuccessfully, it is true; because for some strange reason it wasn't that kind of music. He could sing it a little in his mind, but he couldn't sing either it or *The Raven* out aloud; though when nobody was listening he could and often did sing *Annabel Lee*. All these poems, he was well aware, had been chosen to please *him*; but that was Althea's own fault, because she either never would, or never could, say what she liked. . . .

He gazed up at the bell, hanging motionless and silent beneath the dark rafters framing the roof; and while he did so, slowly it began to take life—the life of a great sleeping, dreaming bat. Yet it was iron—an iron bell—

Every sound that floats
From the rust within their throats
Is a groan.

Tom felt a sudden desire to awaken just one of those groans, but he remembered his promise to Mrs. Fallon, so instead began to repeat the poem, at first into himself, but presently in a chant that grew louder and louder.

And the people—ah, the people—
They that dwell up in the steeple,
All alone. . . .
They are neither man nor woman—
They are neither brute nor human—
They are Ghouls:
And their king it is who tolls;
And he rolls, rolls, rolls,
Rolls
A paean from the bells!
And his merry bosom swells
With the paean of the bells!
And he dances and he yells;
Keeping time, time, time,
In a sort of Runic rhyme,
To the paean of the bells—
Of the bells:
Keeping time, time, time,
In a sort of Runic rhyme,
To the throbbing of the bells—
Of the bells, bells, bells—
To the sobbing of the bells;

Keeping time, time, time,
As he knells, knells, knells,
In a happy Runic rhyme,
To the rolling of the bells—
Of the bells, bells, bells:
To the tolling of the bells,
Of the bells, bells, bells, bells—
Bells, bells, bells—
To the moaning and the groaning of the bells.

The potent magic of that Runic Rhyme had by this time created a kind of intoxication through which he distinctly saw a queer little ancient face surmounted by a pointed cap peeping down at him. It was old, old, old; and it peeped, peeped, peeped—peeping down. It was king of all the people; they that dwelt up in the steeple——But at night?

Tom ceased; suddenly silent at the interruption of another voice.

"Come down, Master Tom. Whatever are you doing up there?"

"Nothing," he shouted in reply. "Just looking."

"Well, it's a queer kind of looking you can hear all over the church. Come along now: I've finished, and I want to lock up."

Mrs. Fallon's tones, though primarily expostulatory, were also distinctly curious; and when he joined her at the foot of the staircase she inspected him with a hint of suspicion in her eye. "You've been up there these twenty minutes or more," she told him; "and there's not a thing to be seen unless it would be a few bats, and you don't see *them* except when they're flying out at night."

"There weren't any bats," Tom admitted. "I mean, I didn't notice any. But it's so dark under the roof there might be hundreds."

"What were you doing then?" Mrs. Fallon persisted. "Not writing your name, I hope—which is what I've known to be done. . . . Names and dates—Roberts and Sarahs—with maybe a heart drew round them, or some such foolery; as if a church was a fitting place for the like of that."

"Still, people get married in church," Tom reminded her. "Anyhow, I didn't write anything: I was just looking at the bell and—thinking."

He gathered up his books, which he had left in one of the pews, and followed by Mrs. Fallon, walked on down the aisle. In the porch he managed to give her yet another surprise, though all he said was; "Could I have the keys, Mrs. Fallon? I mean, would you lend them to me? I'll bring them back to you first thing to-morrow."

Mrs. Fallon gasped—or pretended to. "Well——!" Then she recovered. "And what might you be wanting with the keys, if I may ask?"

"I'd like to come back here by myself. I'll promise not to touch anything or do any harm, and I'll leave them in with you to-morrow morning."

Mrs. Fallon had already thrust the three keys—one large and two smaller—into a capacious pocket, as if she feared he might grab them and run. "Keys!" she said severely. "What would Mr. Sabine think? It's him you'd better be asking for the keys if you want them. Run along home now, like a good boy, and don't be talking your nonsense."

CHAPTER IV

Mrs. Fallon no doubt spoke metaphorically; nevertheless, for a good part of the way, Tom obeyed her literally, having suddenly remembered that Mother had specially asked him not to be late, as Daddy would be coming home for lunch. He strongly suspected that he *was* late, and when, hot and breathless, he burst into the dining-room, suspicion became certainty. He was later even than he had feared. "How often——" But at sight of his flushed face, shining eyes, and the four crimson volumes he dumped down triumphantly on the table between her and Daddy, Mother checked the well-known formula of rebuke at word two. "It's my prize," Tom said, and she looked nearly as pleased as he did himself.

"What—*four* books!" she cried. "Well, I never!"

"It's really only one book," he explained excitedly—"in four series. She had a whole lot of books for me to choose from—*Tom Brown's Schooldays*, *King Solomon's Mines*—oh, heaps and heaps!"

Mother laughed. "So you chose this! If ever there was a little 'curiosity of natural history', I fancy I could name him without much difficulty. . . . No, dear," she hastily added, "I don't mean that, and I'm sure they're most interesting." She turned to the inscription in the first volume and read it aloud, while Daddy took possession of the second.

"It's a prize," Tom whispered to Mary, who had come in, bringing his lunch, which she set before him with a cautionary, "Mind the plate, Master Tom, it'd burn you."

Automatically he advanced an experimental finger, and then began to eat—a somewhat complicated performance, since while doing so he had at the same time to keep a watchful eye on Daddy and Mother, so as not to miss any impression the prize might be producing upon them. Mother's impressions, it is true, were conveyed audibly, by little exclamations and occasional comments and citations, but Daddy required closer observation because he remained silent.

"Who *was* Frank Buckland?" Mother presently asked. "Or should I say who *is* he?"

"He was a naturalist," Daddy replied.

"Yes, I gathered that much myself; but I thought you might know a little more."

"So I do," Daddy answered. "He was Government Inspector of Fisheries, and a popular writer—a kind of journalist-naturalist. It was he who started *Land and Water*, a weekly paper of the same type as *The Field*."

"Miss Sabine says he was like Darwin," Tom put in, but Daddy received this with a non-committal "Hm-m . . .! Darwin was a scientist of the same school as Huxley, and Frank Buckland certainly wasn't that. He was the old-fashioned type of field-naturalist, much more like White of Selborne. . . . But he was a well-known figure in his day, friends with all the keepers in the Zoo, who sometimes sent him smaller animals when they were sick, to be nursed back to health. For that matter, what with monkeys and other pets, his own house must have been very like a zoo in miniature."

"Wasn't he married?" Mother asked, which seemed to Tom an irrelevant question.

"Your mother is thinking of the zoo, Tom. . . . I don't remember whether he was married or not, but if he was, we'll hope the lady shared his tastes, for I've an idea there was an aquarium too."

"I'm going to keep an aquarium," Tom announced, and Mother sighed.

"Yes, I thought that would be the next thing. If you do, you'll keep it either in the garden or the yard. All those creatures sooner or later develop wings, or at any rate become amphibious, and I'm not going to have a lot of nasty insects flying and crawling all over the house."

"Only the beetles get wings," Tom assured her, "and I'm not going to keep beetles; because Max Sabine did, and they killed his sprickleys and ate bits out of them."

"Horrid!" Mother shuddered. "I can't think why boys invariably want to do unpleasant things."

"But it was the beetles," Tom expostulated; and the remark about boys somehow switched his thoughts back to Mrs. Fallon and the stained-glass window. "Who was Ralph Seaford?" he asked.

Mother gazed at him in unfeigned astonishment. "What on earth put Ralph Seaford into your head?"

Daddy, too, looked perplexed; so he had to tell them of his visit to the church, and even then got no satisfactory answer. "Ralph Seaford was just a little boy," Mother said. "The Seaford grave is in the churchyard: you must have seen it often."

"Yes, but what happened to his father and mother? Why didn't *they* put up the window?"

"His father and mother were dead. They were killed in a climbing accident—out in Switzerland. The rope broke, or something. . . . I'm not quite sure what happened."

"I can't say I remember any question of a rope breaking," Daddy put in. "It was never really known *what* happened. They had done the same climb several times with a guide, and it was not considered a particularly dangerous one. . . . This time they did it alone, and it was supposed that one of them may have slipped, and the other fallen in attempting a rescue. Something of the kind at any rate. . . . The boy, Ralph, was only a year or two old at the time, so his grandparents took him to live with them at Tramore."

"At Granny's house?" Tom exclaimed in surprise. "Did you know them?"

Daddy shook his head. "The old people were still living when we first came here, but they both died within that year: Doctor Macrory says they never got over the loss of their grandson. . . .

"After that," Daddy went on reminiscently, "some people called Dickson came to Tramore, but only for six months or so; and the house then stood vacant till Granny took it."

"Against everybody's advice," Mother supplemented.

"Why?" Tom asked; for he liked both the house and the grounds round it; and now the knowledge that it had once belonged to the Seafords lent it an additional interest.

"For one reason, because it's far too big for her," Mother replied. "Certainly nothing would induce *me* to live in a house with a lot of locked-up empty rooms—and servants don't like it either."

But Daddy thought Granny was right. "It's not really such a big house," he said, "and she pays remarkably little for it: the garden alone is worth the rent."

Mother disagreed. "It doesn't come to so little by the time you've paid the wages of two maids and a man. Especially if you're a person like Granny, who gives them all far too much."

Daddy laughed. "Possibly. . . . But if it pleases her, that surely is the main thing. Can you imagine her living happily in a poky little villa with no garden to speak of, and one maid to look after everything?"

"I can imagine her living perfectly happily with us," Mother said, "and it's what I've always wanted her to do."

Daddy shrugged his shoulders. "I think it's much wiser to let people decide these matters for themselves. They're naturally the best judges of what suits them."

"Not always; and it's really only because she hates the idea of parting with any of her possessions. Of course, there wouldn't be room for all her furniture and china and things here——"

"There certainly wouldn't."

"But at least she'd have company. . . . Which reminds me," she went on, turning to Tom, "that she wants *you* to spend a few days with her, now you've got your holidays."

At this sudden and unexpected development, Tom's face grew rather glum. "Days!" he echoed without enthusiasm. He had already made several plans which could only be carried out at home—including this brand-new plan of an aquarium.

"I thought you were so fond of Granny!" Mother reproached him.

"But there's nothing to do there," he responded dolefully. "Granny never does anything, and there's nobody else. . . . Besides," he added, "I can't very well leave the dogs."

It was a perfectly genuine excuse, and he couldn't see why Mother should look displeased, yet she did. "Of course the dogs are a great deal more important than Granny," she said; and since this mild sarcasm elicited no denial; "Surely you can go for a week-end at least! How would *you* like to be left all alone by yourself from morning till night!"

"I'd like it all right," was Tom's artless rejoinder, which, though it made Mother look graver still, drew a characteristic chuckle from Daddy.

A moment's reflection, however, suggested that a week-end meant primarily Sunday, and after all, it didn't much matter *where* you were on Sundays, so he changed his mind and asked, "When?"

Mother's face cleared. She made a rapid calculation. "Let me see. To-day is Tuesday. You could go on Friday or Saturday."

Here Daddy intervened. "He can't go on Friday. I called to see Mr. Pemberton this morning, and he wants him to sit for an examination on Friday."

"An examination!" Mother cried. "When he's not even at school yet!"

"This is for the boys who will be going after the summer. It gives him some idea of how much they know and in what form to put them. . . . In the present case, the very highest, I should think, judging from those four splendid volumes now before us!"

Glancing at Mother, Tom saw that though Daddy had spoken jestingly some such idea had crossed her own mind, therefore he hastened to nip any hopes she might be entertaining in the bud. "There'll be far older boys than me there," he told her; but instead of corroborating this, Daddy questioned it. "Most of them will be younger," he declared. "Some only eight or nine, and you're eleven. Anyhow, I should think you'd be graded according to your ages."

Tom at once switched on to another track. "Does it matter if I don't do well?" he asked; and was relieved when Daddy answered, "Not in the least," before Mother had quite time to get out, "Of course it matters." Unfortunately she also said: "I'm sure you *will* do well."

He sighed, for that was just the difficulty. And Miss Sabine would be surer still. He looked up to find Mother's eyes fixed upon him with an odd expression, half amused, and to that extent reassuring. Daddy had ceased to be interested and had taken a sheaf of papers from his pocket.

"Well, we needn't discuss what is still in the future," Mother concluded, rising from the table. "And don't look as if all the cares of the world were on your shoulders: Daddy has just told you it doesn't matter how you do. I don't quite know why—but there it is." She passed behind him, laughed, and stooping down, kissed him on the top of his head.

CHAPTER V

The cares of the world, however, slipped from him like Christian's Burden, as he left Daddy to his papers and went out into the garden. The more immediate care was to find a suitable place for an aquarium. As for the aquarium itself, there was an old bath up in the loft which he thought might do, so he went round to the yard and climbed the ladder to have a look at it. He knew, of course, that to be really satisfactory an aquarium ought to be made of glass. He had seen a picture of one, and it stood on a kind of trestle, and was square, with glass sides through which you could see all that was going on within. Max Sabine had used a goldfish-bowl, but that would be much too small for what he wanted. Anyhow, he hadn't got one, so the bath would have to do.

He dragged it out now from its corner for inspection, and removed a festoon of cobwebs. The enamel inside was cracked, and the outside was coated with rust, but that didn't matter so long as it didn't leak, and he could see no holes when with some difficulty he tilted it up against the light. He had already evolved a plan which seemed quite practicable. He would dig a trench beside the shrubbery, just deep enough to contain the bath, and in this way turn it into a little pond, with the upper rim of the bath flush with the soil, or perhaps an inch or two above it. . . . Only he wished it was deeper. Then it would be exactly like a natural pool, with the grass growing round it.

All this would require to be done very neatly and accurately, the sods cut out and the edges trimmed with a sharp spade. The best way would be to place the bath upside down on the grass, and get somebody to sit on it to keep it from moving while he cut round it: after that the rest should be easy.

Unfortunately, he would have to ask William to help him to get it down. And William would grumble, being made that way. But if he let him grumble for a while, and didn't answer back, in the end he might do what was wanted. Tom had reached this point when a sudden doubt arose in his mind. It had nothing to do with the construction of the aquarium; that was all settled; but when it *was* made, wouldn't the dogs use it? They had got into the habit of taking it for granted that whatever he did was done for them, and Barker, especially, could never resist water in any shape or form. In imagination, Tom could see him now, slopping about in the middle of the aquarium, perhaps lying down in it, and at any rate scaring all its legitimate inhabitants to death. Stray cats, too, from Denny's farm, where there were swarms of them, might fish in it at night. The glen was their usual hunting-ground, but he was sure they visited the garden as well; in fact he had often heard them; and fish were to cats what water was to Barker. . . .

He wished he knew some other boy who was interested in aquariums and would help him. As it was, there was only Max Sabine, his enemy, whom he disliked more than ever after what Althea had told him, though he had always known he was slimy and treacherous. If only James-Arthur wasn't kept so busy at the farm he would have been the very person. . . .

Undecided, he descended from the loft and came round again to the front of the house, where he found Daddy seated patiently in the car, waiting to drive Mother into town. Tom stood by the door, and as soon as she appeared asked if he might come too, though he already knew she had an appointment with the hairdresser and after that was going to have tea at the McFerrans', where Daddy was to call for her a little before six to bring her home. But his request was merely formal, and having watched them depart, he fetched the croquet-balls and a mallet from the hall and began a solitary game, blue and black against red and yellow.

Now of all games, croquet is the least amusing when played alone. Tom began this one with every intention of finishing it, but "whether skill prevailed" (which was seldom) "or happy blunder triumphed" (infrequent also) it was equally dull, and after ten minutes or so he gave it up and returned to the house to get his yacht.

Between the cloak-room door and the grandfather's clock,

stood a big oak chest in which the croquet and tennis things, with a few of his more personal belongings, were kept. Here was his yacht, and he lifted it out, gazed at it, and put it back again, taking a much smaller boat instead—one he could easily carry tucked under his arm. Then he set off for the river, visiting on his way the raspberry canes to see if any raspberries were ripe. He found only two or three rather dubious specimens, but he ate them, before taking the path through the shrubbery, at the end of which was a green postern door where two walls of the garden joined. Passing through this door, he was immediately above the glen, on the top of a high steep bank thickly carpeted with dark glossy bluebell-leaves. In spring, this bank was a feast of brilliant colour, but there were no flowers now, except here and there the small white flowers of a few wild strawberries. A narrow path bordered by nettles ran along the top of the bank, but Tom clambered down to the stream and followed that.

The slender trees were nearly all either larch or birch or hazel, and the sun, glinting between them, was the colour of old silver. He now began to realize how hot it was—actually hotter down here in the shade than it had been up above in the open sunshine, for the air was heavier, almost stagnant. The birds were silent; a low droning murmur, which accompanied and mingled with the splash of water, proceeded from smaller winged creatures.

Gradually the banks of the glen widened out as Tom neared its entrance, and presently he emerged into a flat meadow-land. Here the stream was broader and shallower, flowing between beds of flowering rushes. In winter, after a rainy spell, this land became a swamp; and even now, though dry enough, it was soft as velvet beneath his feet. The whole meadow was flooded with brilliant sunlight, but in the distance everything melted into a bluish-silver haze, composed of air and cloud and sky.

A solitary tree grew in the meadow—an oak. It must once have been a giant, for though now its branches were sadly dwindled, the girth of the trunk was immense. Tom knew it well, because Edward, the squirrel, lived here. It was quite hollow, and many of the branches had broken off and fallen, though those remaining still put forth leaves and, at the right time of the year, a crop of acorns. The boughs were so brittle that it was a dangerous tree to climb, but James-Arthur had climbed it, and said the trunk was quite hollow and looked just like a huge chimney; so that if you were to slip and fall down inside you would never be heard of again, but would gradually starve to death, unless somebody passing by happened to hear your cries. . . .

Leaving his boat by the stream, Tom ran over to the oak and whistled, but apparently Edward was not at home. He knew Tom's whistle quite well, and if he had been there he certainly would have peeped out on the chance that a few nuts had been brought to him. Tom had in fact brought him some biscuits, only there was no use leaving these, as, what with mice and other creatures, it was most unlikely they would still be there when Edward came back. . . .

Half-way up the trunk, a bat hung motionless and asleep, with his dark wings neatly folded. Tom had never before seen one sleeping right out in the open, and he wondered whether he ought to awaken him or not. He must be a very young and inexperienced bat, or he would have known that the cats from Denny's were always prowling about, and might easily come as far as this on the chance of picking up a baby rabbit. On the other hand, he couldn't be reached except by throwing a stick or a stone, and he was sure bats were very easily hurt. He returned to the stream therefore, and picking up the boat, continued on his way. . . .

At the end of the meadow was a deep ditch, with thickets of brambles on one side and a steep bank surmounted by a hedge on the other. In the hedge were more brambles, and a tangle of wild roses now in full bloom and stretching wide their pink and white petals to drink in the heat. But the ditch was dry, so in spite of the thorns that caught at his jacket and tried to hold him, Tom was able to wriggle his way through, emerging on to the tow-path between two bends of the river, whose winding course could be traced by the trees on the farther bank.

Kneeling at the water's edge, he fixed the rudder of his boat to steer a slanting course to the opposite shore. When it was nearing land he would cross over himself by the lock gate, which, though out of sight, was not more than fifty yards beyond the nearer bend. But it was a bad day for sailing boats. A languid puff of air caught the sails for a moment or two, and this, with the push he had given it, carried the boat out towards mid-stream, where it began to drift slowly with the current. Tom followed it along the bank till it reached a clump of water-lilies; yet, though it only brushed them, in the lack of wind this was sufficient, and there it remained—"as idle as a painted ship upon a painted ocean".

He searched for a stone to throw at it, because it was not even entangled, and beyond this one snag had a perfectly clear passage. But there were no stones big enough to be of any use, so he sat down on the bank, since there was nothing else to do.

The broad shining lily-leaves cast black shadows on the water. The yellow flowers were as usual half closed, and a dragon-fly was dreaming on one of them, his blue enamelled body glittering in the sun. In a very few minutes Tom was dreaming himself. He didn't really care whether the boat worked loose or not, for toys had never interested him much. When he got a present of one he would play with it for a shorter or longer period, but that first experiment over, he would put it away and very seldom think of it again. The model yacht, for instance, had been a present from Granny on his last birthday, and after a single trial had rarely been removed from the chest in the hall. If Granny had given him a monkey, now—as he had himself suggested—or indeed anything alive—but a model yacht! He was glad, at all events, that he had left it at home to-day, for it didn't matter a straw whether this other old boat were lost or not. . . .

Suddenly he heard a faint splash on the opposite side of the river, and instantly boats were forgotten. He knew what *that* was, and next moment fancied he could see the very small head, and certainly could see the ripple in the water behind it. Daddy had told him there were no real water-rats in Ireland, but there were at least plenty of rats who lived near the river and appeared to be more or less amphibious. This one was swimming straight across to him. Perhaps he had not seen him, and would change his direction when he did; yet on he came, nearer and nearer, and soon it was quite clear that he was making directly for Tom, for his black little beads of eyes were inspecting him very sharply indeed. In another minute he had scrambled out of the water and up the bank, where he sat down and proceeded to comb his whiskers.

Tom had an impulse to dry him with his pocket handkerchief, only he thought the rat perhaps liked being wet, and at any rate, with his short fur, the sun would dry him in no time. Then he remembered something much better—the biscuits he had brought for Edward—most attractive-looking biscuits, with pink and white sugar on the top. He put his hand in his pocket and fumbled; but alas! when he fished the biscuits out, they were in a sadly broken condition and all mixed up with sand. That, of course, must have happened when he was getting through the hedge, squirming his way through on his stomach.

Luckily the rat did not seem to mind. One by one he took each piece of biscuit in his tiny hands and nibbled it quite nicely. Not that this surprised Tom, for he knew rats, like squirrels, had better table-manners than most animals. It was really because they *had* hands, he supposed; since without hands, table-manners must be rather a problem.

"I was glad to see you had no dogs with you to-day," the rat said presently, and Tom noticed that he was careful not to speak with his mouth full. "So I thought I'd seize the opportunity, for it's not often you're without them."

"No," Tom replied.

"Which is a pity," the rat went on, "because it must greatly narrow the circle of your friends."

This hadn't occurred to Tom before, yet when the rat mentioned it he felt that very likely he *was* associated with dogs in the minds of other animals. "You see," he hastened to explain, "I'm very fond of them: we're old friends."

"Lovers, I should call it," the rat answered unsympathetically. "At least so far as the one with the brush is concerned."

"The brush?" Tom repeated, momentarily puzzled. "Oh,

you mean his tail. . . . But it's not a brush: it's far more like a big feather."

"Well, a feather-brush," the rat said.

"That's Roger," Tom told him; "and you'd like him. At least if you could once make friends with him you would: and I'm sure you could if I was there."

"The little one's the worst," the rat went on dispassionately.

"Pincher?"

"Yes, I dare say he'd be called that. . . . The old lazy one's the best."

"Barker?"

The rat seemed amused. "Ridiculous names, all of them," he sniggered, "but then they're ridiculous creatures. What, if I may ask, is your own name? Squeaker, perhaps?"

"Squeaker's much more like yourself," Tom retorted indignantly, for whatever his table-manners might be, the rat's politeness appeared to end there. "I don't squeak."

"You're squeaking now," the rat said. "And anyhow, don't lose your temper."

"I haven't lost my temper; but I think you might be a little more civil—especially after gobbling up all the biscuits."

To his surprise, the rat took this quite well. "I enjoyed the biscuits," he admitted, looking rather ashamed. "Didn't I thank you for them? At any rate I enjoyed them very much indeed. One often hears of such things, but seldom sees them. You may be surprised to learn that I'd never tasted a biscuit before in my life. . . . And please don't misunderstand me," he continued, delicately removing a crumb from his whiskers. "It's universally granted that you're a most agreeable little boy—much above the average. Indeed, I may say that you're regarded as practically unique. We all think that. Your actual name, however, has caused a good deal of dispute and conjecture. You're usually referred to as the Child, or the Boy, or Freckles, or Snub Nose, or——"

"You needn't go on with the list," Tom interrupted him. "My name is Tom."

"And a very good name too," the rat declared encouragingly.

"The best names, as I'm sure you've noticed, are always in one syllable—like Rat, Mouse, Frog, Bat, Horse, Pig, Cow—and now we can add Tom."

"And Dog, and Cat, and Owl," Tom was continuing, but the rat looked displeased. "I don't think we need include those," he said coldly. "There are exceptions to every rule."

"There are a jolly lot to yours," Tom agreed. "What about Squirrel? You can't possibly object to him. And Badger, and Otter, and——" But whether Rat would have objected or not he was never to learn, for at that moment they both heard the tramp of approaching footsteps, and in a flash Tom was alone.

The tramp, tramp, tramp, was made by heavy boots, and in time to a martial tune, which in spite of elaborate variations Tom recognized as "Onward Christian Soldiers". Next moment the Christian Soldier himself appeared round the bend of the river, waving his banner, a towel.

"Where are you going?" Tom demanded, for it was only James-Arthur from the farm.

"Goin' for a dip," James-Arthur replied. "Oul' Denny let me off." Then he saw the boat. "You've got her well stuck there! Sure, what was the use of tryin' to sail her a day like that? She'll be there now till night unless you go in for her."

"I can't go in for her," Tom answered, "and you know I can't."

James-Arthur reflected, for he did know it.

"*You* can swim," Tom said. "You're a good swimmer."

"Not so bad," James-Arthur confessed modestly. "An' if you like to come along with me, I'm just goin' down below the weir."

"If you bathed here you could get the boat," Tom said pointedly.

But James-Arthur only scratched a flaxen poll and shuffled his feet. He was, however, a most good-natured boy, and presently he murmured doubtfully; "I wouldn't like, Master Tom."

"Why?" Tom asked. He knew, of course, that the water below the weir, where the current was strong, was much cleaner and fresher, but he didn't see why James-Arthur couldn't go in here first.

James-Arthur, nevertheless, continued to look worried. "Well —someone might come along," he explained. "It'd be all right for a wee lad like you; but if I was to take off me on the bank here someone might come along."

"You said that before," Tom told him. "What matter if they do come along? You're only a boy yourself."

James-Arthur shook his head, though clearly wavering. "Ah now," he mumbled, "sure you know it wouldn't be the same at all. They might be making a complaint. I'm sixteen, and bigger'n you—about twiced—an' it might be a woman too."

"It won't be anybody," Tom returned impatiently; for this bashfulness seemed to him extremely silly. He himself, like most small boys, was perfectly indifferent to nakedness. "I've been here for hours," he went on, "and there hasn't been a soul, except a rat—not even a barge. . . . Anyhow," he wound up persuasively, "I'll promise to keep watch; and I'll shout the moment I see anyone, and you can stay in the water till they've gone by."

Yet even with this assurance James-Arthur did not look too happy. In his mind there was evidently a conflict going on between a sense of propriety and his liking for Tom. In the end, but with obvious reluctance, he gave in; and sat down on the bank to remove his boots and socks. The rest did not take him long, for it consisted only of a dirty ragged old pair of flannel trousers and a grey flannel shirt.

James-Arthur was as fond of the water as Barker, and now, while he stood up on the bank in the sunlight, he slapped his sturdy thighs in pleased anticipation. Even at this early date of summer his body was sunburnt, and in Tom's eyes he somehow did not look naked. He had simply emerged from his soiled and much-patched clothing like a butterfly from a chrysalis, and the contrast between his fair hair and the golden brown of his body and limbs appeared to the smaller boy as attractive as anything could be. In fact James-Arthur, merely by divesting himself of his clothes, had instantly become part of the natural scene, like the grass and the trees and the river and the sky, and the dragon-fly asleep upon his water-lily. Tom told him how nice he looked, and, while James-Arthur only smiled and said he was a queer wee lad, it was easy to see that secretly he was not displeased.

Anyhow, he plunged in, rescued the boat (which was the main thing), and then swam quietly about for a bit, very much in Barker's manner.

Watching him, Tom felt more and more tempted to go in too. "Is it cold?" he shouted.

"Naw; it's not cold:—how would it be cold, and the sun on it all these days?"

Tom, nevertheless, felt pretty certain that *he* would find it cold. Yet James-Arthur appeared to be enjoying himself so much that he made up his mind and hurriedly undressed.

"Wait now," James-Arthur called out. "Don't be comin' in without me. There's deep holes—plenty of them—would take you over your head in a minute."

He swam to the bank, and gingerly Tom stepped into the water. At the edge it rose hardly above his knees, but a single pace forward and he was floundering in one of those very holes, from which James-Arthur rescued him, spluttering and gasping.

James-Arthur laughed, but Tom, as he tried to spit out the far from crystalline water he had swallowed, saw nothing to laugh at. "Lie flat on your belly, Master Tom. Don't be afeared: I'll keep your head up."

Having complete confidence in his instructor, Tom obeyed; but as he had suspected it *was* cold, except on the surface.

"Easy on, now," James-Arthur encouraged him. "Take your time, an' go slow. You've watched the frogs many's a time: try an' kick your arms and legs out what they do. . . . That's fine now: you'll be the great swimmer yet."

And when they came out he made Tom take the towel, while to dry himself he used only his flannel trousers. "How did you like it?" he asked, with a broad grin.

"It was very nice," Tom temporized. "At least, I think perhaps I'd get to like it."

"Course you would," James-Arthur said.

"Only," Tom added, wrinkling up his nose, "I've got a smell, and it's pretty strong—the smell of the water."

"Ah, sure that's nothin'. A bit nifty maybe till you get used to it, but it'll pass off in the course of the evening."

"I hope so," Tom said, for he didn't think James-Arthur realized the full potency of the "niftiness". "I saw your mother this morning," he went on. "She let me go up the tower."

"Ay, she was tellin' me so; an' that you were wantin' the keys off her. . . . But I'll have to leave you now, Master Tom. Oul' Denny only give me half an hour an' it's more like an hour I've bin."

He caught up his towel, gave Tom an amicable slap on the shoulder, and departed—once more to the strains of "Onward Christian Soldiers".

CHAPTER VI

Tom sat on alone. He had been very happy a few minutes ago, but now that James-Arthur was gone he felt sad. He thought he would like to be a farm boy at Denny's, working every day with James-Arthur; instead of which he was going to school, and all he knew about school was what Max Sabine had told him, obviously with the view of showing what an important person he was there, which Tom didn't for a moment believe.

Cloppity clop! Cloppity clop!

He looked up, and saw a big grey barge horse approaching. Next minute the barge itself came into sight, the rope slackening as it rounded the bend; then suddenly tightening again, rippling through the water and throwing up a shower of spray. A man was walking beside the horse; another man was at the tiller.

Tom drew back to be out of the way. He was prepared to nod to both men and return their greeting, but beyond an indifferent and somewhat surly glance, neither took any notice of him, and they and the horse and the barge passed on just as if he were non-existent, presently disappearing from view round the next bend. Why couldn't they have said something? Then he too would have walked beside the horse and kept the man company for a little way, and perhaps told him about bathing. . . .

He had stooped to lift his boat, when suddenly he was sent staggering nearly on to his nose by the impact of a warm heavy body against the middle of his back, while simultaneously two big paws were planted on his shoulders. It was Roger, who had come up silently behind him. He was always playing these tricks—more like a boy than a dog—and immediately Tom's cheerfulness was restored. Roger licked his face, so he licked Roger—but just once, because he had been told it was a disgusting thing to do. It couldn't be disgusting, however, unless there was somebody there to be disgusted, and at present there was no one.

"Well, I suppose *you'll* want to bathe now!" Tom said, adopting an elderly manner. "But it'll be only one dip and then out, for it must be time to go home. Where have you been, and how did you guess I was here?"

Roger, instead of answering, began to bark and jump about him, rushing to the edge of the bank and back, slewing round his head, and making it very clear in every way what he expected Tom to do. But there were no sticks on the tow-path, and bits of hedge were far too light to carry any distance. In the end, Tom seized his boat by the mast, and pitched it out as far as he could. Before it had even left his hand, Roger leapt into the water, making a tremendous splash, calculated to scare Rat out of his wits if he were still lurking in the neighbourhood. As he watched him swimming smoothly and swiftly, Tom wished Roger had come sooner, for then he could have had a race with James-Arthur. They had very different styles of swimming, and James-Arthur declared that even in a short race across the river and back Roger wouldn't have a chance; but if James-Arthur used the breast stroke and gave Roger half a minute's start Tom wasn't so sure. . . .

The boat was floating on its side when Roger reached it. He made a grab at the hull, but it was too big for him to get a proper grip, so he bit on the mast and sails and struggled along that way—though not without difficulty, to judge by the growls and snorts. He couldn't be really angry, of course, but it sounded as if he were, and Tom hopped about shouting encouragement mingled with laughter. It was an extremely wrecked-looking boat which eventually was dragged up the bank and dropped at his feet. He didn't care. "Good dog!" he said, hastily stepping back to avoid a shower-bath. "And now I *must* go home: I was late for lunch, and you should have come sooner if you wanted to bathe." He picked up the wreck, and they returned by the route James-Arthur had taken.

As it happened, he needn't have been in such a hurry; in fact he had been waiting on the doorstep for nearly half an hour, and Phemie had twice appeared to remark that the dinner would be ruined, before the car drove up with Daddy and Mother. "I know we're very late," Mother called out through the window. "I expect you're starving and Phemie is furious, but it couldn't be helped. . . . You'll find a parcel on the back seat which you might take into the house. It's a book Granny ordered; and it cost five guineas, so be very careful with it. Why she should want to spend a fortune on a huge tome about Chinese art is best known to herself."

"Japanese, I expect," Daddy amended.

"Well—Chinese or Japanese—five guineas seems to me an absurd price. It nearly took my breath away when the man told me."

"Special publications of that kind are always expensive," Daddy said. "The pictures very likely are printed in facsimile. . . . What is the correct name for a book of that size?" he suddenly asked Tom, who stood clasping it in his arms.

"A folio," Tom replied learnedly. "May I look at it: the string's untied."

"Did *you* untie it?" Mother questioned suspiciously, but added; "Perhaps—if you're very good—after dinner. . . . Only you must promise to take the greatest care and your hands must be spotless."

"They're spotless now," Tom informed her. "I've been bathing."

Mother might have inquired further into this unexpected disclosure had not Phemie at that moment again appeared in the doorway, her countenance this time suggesting that there were limits even to *her* patience. So it was not till they were safely seated at the dinner-table that he was able to embark on a fuller description of his adventures. Mother was not enthusiastic about the bathing part, and made him promise not to do it again without first getting her permission, and never to do it at all unless James-Arthur was there to look after him. But she was amused by the behaviour of the rat, and thus encouraged, Tom in the end produced a few specimens of their conversation.

Mother maintained that all rats were horrid, and some of them evidently most conceited; while Daddy went on quietly with his dinner and did not appear to be listening. This, as it turned out, was a delusion, for suddenly he said: "It seems to me Miss Sabine was definitely right, and that it's high time you went to school."

There followed a pause, before Mother replied rather dryly; "If rats choose to talk to Tom, I can't see how that is any concern of Miss Sabine's."

"Yes—*if*," Daddy agreed.

A faint flush rose in Mother's cheeks. "Judging from all accounts, school doesn't appear to have particularly improved her own nephew," she said.

The matter dropped there, for Daddy returned no answer, and during the remainder of dinner Mother too spoke little, and then merely on the dullest matters of fact. By the time they rose from the table it was well after eight and within half an hour of Tom's bedtime.

Daddy, who had so effectually, if perhaps unintentionally, thrown a damper on the conversation, now followed his usual custom and went out to potter about the garden, while Mother retired to the kitchen to discuss household matters with Phemie. Tom, alone in the study, vacillated between the rival attractions of *Curiosities of Natural History* and Granny's book. It might be better to choose Granny's, he decided, since very likely she would either send or call for it to-morrow; so placing it carefully on the table, he drew up a chair and began to turn the pages.

Daddy had at least been right about the pictures; they *were* coloured, and most of them were queer—some of them very queer indeed. There were birds and animals, and pre-eminent among the latter was a superb tiger, with his head lowered and an extraordinary expression on his face. Whatever might be true of rats, it was at least quite clear that *he* could talk, and also that he could come alive and spring right out of the book if he wanted to. Tom was fascinated by this picture, yet at the same time wasn't wholly sure that he would have liked to have it hanging above his bed. . . . That is, unless he could make friends with it first. . . Then it would be lovely. . . . "Puss—puss," he whispered, as a preliminary endearment.

But there were men and women, too, and they were equally strange—even the more ordinary ones—with their slanting eyes and pale, mask-like faces; to say nothing of the demons, bogeys, and magicians. Mother, entering unnoticed, found him absorbed, with flushed cheeks and very bright eyes, while a single rapid glance at the picture he was studying showed her how foolish she had been not first to have had a look at Granny's book herself. She gently drew it away from him, and he relinquished it without a word: nor did she say anything except that he could come for a little walk round the garden with her before going to bed.

He was surprised, for a glance at the clock told him it was already past his bedtime, but he asked no questions, and they went out together into the evening twilight. The garden was dreamy and still; pleasanter, because cooler, than it had been all day. Daddy, surrounded by a halo of moths, was doing something with his sweet-peas, and looked up to greet them. Then he stooped to capture an imprudent snail, while Tom and Mother passed slowly on, her hand resting lightly on his shoulder.

She talked gaily of any topic she thought might at once distract and tranquillize his mind, but all the time she was secretly reproaching herself. For she had seen his face as it was raised from Granny's book, and though a tendency to walk in his sleep appeared to have little connection with any immediate or discoverable cause, Doctor Macrory had strongly urged that there should be no pre-bedtime excitements. Of course it was most unreasonable to feel vexed with Granny, when the fault was entirely her own; nevertheless she *did* feel vexed; and determined to have a look at the other pictures after Tom had gone to bed, in the hope that they might prove more innocent than the horribly malevolent and lifelike demon he had been poring over when she had discovered him. One good thing was, that his nocturnal peregrinations nearly always took place early—before she and Daddy had retired. To-night she would sit up later than usual, and must be sure to leave her bedroom door open, which occasionally she forgot to do.

CHAPTER VII

Yet, had he guessed her anxiety, Tom could have told her that there wasn't the slightest danger of his walking in his sleep, and this for the excellent reason that he had a plan which necessitated lying awake. True, a most important part of the plan had been defeated by Mrs. Fallon's refusal to lend him the keys, but he could still pay a midnight visit to the church, even if he could not go inside. Therefore it was in a way disappointing to find he no longer very much wanted to pay this visit. The attractiveness of the adventure had curiously waned with the waning of daylight, and at present he was positively glad that Mrs. Fallon had been so scrupulous. With the keys in his possession, he might have felt it his duty to make use of them, whereas now—supposing he went at all—he need only look over the wall from the road. . . .

But that "supposing" was nonsense: of course he was going: he had said he was, and though nobody had heard him and therefore nobody knew, to back out at this stage would be none the less to funk it—at the thought of which the lines of his mouth grew remarkably obstinate.

In fact it seemed hardly worth while undressing—except that

Mother occasionally came in to see him after he was in bed, and she would be sure to notice if he still had his clothes on. Besides, with such an exploit looming before him, he wasn't in the least likely to fall asleep, and to make doubly sure, he would lie and think about his aquarium. Then, when all the house was quiet, he would start.

Once snugly in bed, however, he felt less adventurous than ever, though not a bit drowsy. He lay on his back, his eyes wide open, thinking first of his aquarium, and then of the examination on Friday, when he would see a lot of boys he had never seen before. Even if there were only a few, there might still be one with whom he could make friends. At least, that was always what happened in school stories. In the very first chapter—or if not in the first, at any rate in the second—the hero always found a chum; and, though he would have liked to be, of course he wasn't really James-Arthur's chum. James-Arthur, when his work was over, went about with boys of his own age, and now and then—which was more surprising—with girls. . . .

Mother evidently wasn't coming, but she had done what was much the same thing, she had gone to the drawing-room and begun to sing. It was for him, he guessed, or partly for him, and she had left the door open so that he might listen, for she knew that this was what he liked. He himself could sing most of her songs, and did, not only at the piano but all over the house. When Miss Sabine was there he was invariably called on to perform, but not when there was only Doctor Macrory, because Doctor Macrory, like Daddy, couldn't tell one tune from another.

I remember all you told me,
Looking out where we did stand,
While the night flowers poured their perfume
Forth like stars from——"

The song Mother was singing was called "Edenland". The tune had a waltz rhythm, which the accompaniment accentuated, so that it seemed to swing round and round inside you, rising at the end of each verse to a climax before dying away. In silence Tom's body moved now with this mounting climax——

And the path where we two wandered,
And the path where we two wandered,
Seemed not like earth, but Edenland,
Seemed not like earth, like earth,
But Edenland.

Mother sang song after song, picking out his favourites——

I think of all thou art to me,
I dream of what thou canst not be,
My life is filled with thoughts of thee,
Forever and forever.

Actually it should have been "My life is cursed with thoughts of thee", but Mother had crossed out "cursed" and written "filled" above it. . . . He hoped she would sing "When Sparrows Build"; but these were the introductory bars of "My dearest Heart", also a favourite——

All the dreaming is broken through,
Both what is done and undone I rue,
Nothing is steadfast, nothing is true,
But your love for me, and my love for you,
My dearest, dearest heart.

There were three verses to Arthur Sullivan's song, and when it was finished, Mother was silent for a long while—so long that he began to think she must have stopped altogether. But he was wrong; she hadn't; and now there came at last what he had been waiting for——

When sparrows build, and the leaves break forth,
My old sorrow wakes and cries,
For I know there is dawn in the far, far north,
And a scarlet sun doth rise;
Like a scarlet fleece the snow-field spreads,
And the icy founts run free,
And the bergs begin to bow their heads,
And plunge and sail in the sea.

O my lost love, and my own, own love,
And my love that loved me so!
Is there never a chink in the world above
Where they listen to words from below?
Nay, I spoke once, and I grieved thee sore,
I remember all that I said,
And now thou wilt hear me no more—no more
Till the sea gives up her dead.

* * * * *

We shall walk no more through the sodden plain
With the faded bents o'erspread;
We shall stand no more by the seething main
While the dark wrack drives o'erhead;
We shall part no more in the wind and the rain,
Where thy last farewell was said;
But perhaps I shall meet thee and know thee again
When the sea gives up her dead.

After that, he did not know how many more songs Mother sang, for he must have fallen asleep in the middle of one of them, and when he opened his eyes the night was gone, the sun was shining in at his window, and somewhere down below, Roger was barking. In a trice Tom was out of bed and hurriedly dressing. Out in the garden Roger greeted him with effusion, tore wildly round the lawn in a circle, and then, with Tom after him, raced on to the gate.

It was a lovely morning—cloudless, cool, and fresh—the air extraordinarily clear. But it was impossible to keep up with Roger, who dashed on ahead, and quickly was out of sight round the bend of the road. Well, he could just come back again, Tom thought, and slackened his pace to a walk. It was only then that in the hedge, a few yards farther on, a door he had never before noticed was suddenly pushed open, and a girl looked out and beckoned to him. Tom did not know her, had never seen her before, and he stood gazing at her without either advancing or retreating. It was not that he was shy of strangers as a general rule, but this girl was so different from anybody he had ever met, or expected to meet, that he forgot his manners. For one thing, her skin was smooth as ivory, and pale yellow: for another, she had narrow dark eyes set obliquely under thin, slanting eyebrows; and her sleek black hair was drawn tightly back and rolled up on the top of her head. Her mouth was extremely small; her nose was rather long, and curved down to a point, almost like a parrot's beak. Her dress was equally unusual, for it was gathered about her in loose voluminous folds that appeared to cling to her without any visible fastening. Moreover it was brilliantly blue and green and white, sprinkled all over with embroidered flowers, and she carried in her left hand a little fan. Certainly she was attractive, in a strange exotic fashion that seemed to him about three-quarters human. But this first, somewhat dubious impression lasted only till she spoke, when he immediately regained confidence; for her voice was beautiful—low and clear like a wood-pigeon's—as she invited him to come in and look at her garden.

She spoke and smiled so pleasantly that he couldn't very well refuse, though really he wanted to go after Roger, who hadn't returned, which was most unlike him. But he need only stay a minute or two, she told him; a single glance would show him what the garden was like; couldn't he spare just a moment?—and her eyes glinted oddly over the fluttering fan.

Still doubtful, yet by no means incurious, Tom followed her into the brightest, gayest garden he had ever beheld—composed entirely of flowering shrubs, with vivid emerald-green patches of smooth short grass, stone terraces, and tiny ponds; while in the midst of all was a stone house, carved and ornamented like a huge ivory casket, and surmounted by a tower. He thought it very wonderful—that at least was his first reaction; his second, perhaps, that the garden was too perfectly arranged and elaborately ornamental to be really *his* kind of garden. And the house, with its carved dragons and delicate arabesques and tracery, was equally artificial. But he could hardly tell her this, though quite evidently she was waiting for his opinion. So he expressed a thought suggested by the numerous little ponds and pools: "What a lot of aquariums you could have!"

He feared it might not be quite the remark she expected, yet she seemed pleased, and agreed at once. "Yes, goldfish, and silver fish, and water-lilies. . . . Only now you *are* here, you must come in and be introduced to my brothers. They are just going to have supper."

For an instant, at the sound of that incongruous last word, the whole garden seemed to flicker like a candle-flame in the wind—to flicker and go out. Or did it?—for he was walking up the path with her, they were entering the house.

There, in a big bright room with many windows, the three brothers were already seated at the table, but they were much older than he had expected—short, fat men, nearly naked too, with yellow faces and thin drooping black moustaches. And protruding slightly beneath each moustache were two pointed walrus tusks, very sharp and cruel-looking. That they were magicians, Tom recognized immediately, and he did not like their appearance at all. Nor, for that matter, did he now like the strangely sly and altered smile with which the girl was watching him. He had seen a cat watching a bird just like that, and with a sinking of the heart he felt he had better go away at once, and said so.

Since he had entered the room the brothers had not opened their lips nor even looked at him, but now one of them spoke, in a smooth, expressionless voice—"Isn't it too late to think of that?"—and instantly Tom knew it *was* too late, and that he would never leave that house alive.

He made an effort to reach the still open door, and none of them moved or spoke, merely watched his struggles. For he could do nothing; all the strength had gone out from him, and his feet seemed to be glued to the floor. But at that moment, just as he realized that he was indeed lost and helpless, there came from far, far away, yet distinctly audible in the silent room, the sound of a dog barking.

Though infinitely faint and distant, nevertheless it was Roger's bark, and it had an instantaneous effect on the inmates of the room. The eyes of the seated brothers slid round quickly towards the windows, the power flowed back into Tom's limbs, while the girl gave him an evil look and said contemptuously: "Now, I suppose, he must get his chance."

Tom hated her. He hated her even more than he hated the magicians; because it was she who had decoyed him in and betrayed him. And though she seemed so young, that, too, must be an illusion, she must really be an old hag, as old as her brothers, and all four probably had made many a meal off tender and juicy small boys whom she had entrapped—serving them up whole, very likely—and in their skins—like baked potatoes.

All the same, his courage had revived with his strength, and above all with the certainty he now felt that Roger, wherever he was, had missed him, had divined his peril, and was at this moment trying to get back to him, to break through whatever magic barrier of intervening space the magicians had created by their spells.

He was to have a chance, they had said: but what kind of chance? They soon told him, and he was relieved; indeed now felt very little alarm. All he had to do was to climb the three flights of steps, which would bring him out on to the roof of the tower, before the girl—who would start level with him—had climbed them three times. True, the trial also was to be repeated three times; but with such an enormous start surely he had nothing to fear.

And it turned out to be even easier than he had expected. At the given signal, a sharp blow on a gong, they both started together from the hall, and though she was certainly quicker than he, and to gain the roof he had to hoist himself through an open trap-door, yet he had done so, and come out on to the square stone platform at the top, before she had half finished her second ascent. Looking over the parapet, he now saw far below him, not the wonderful garden, but a wide, bare landscape—stretching out and out—with, on the extreme edge of it, yet nevertheless *within* it, a tiny black spot which he somehow knew to be Roger.

Well, that was over, and it had been nothing; he wasn't even out of breath, he wouldn't mind a dozen such races. So it was in a spirit of complete confidence that he started on the second trial. This time he did not exert himself so much—or was it, perhaps, that the girl exerted herself more? for he was a little startled when she actually passed him on her second ascent before he had reached the roof. Looking again over the parapet, he found that the landscape had greatly contracted, and that Roger was quite close—close enough to bark an excited recognition, with frantic waggings of his whole body. Tom called down to him, and braced himself, this time in dead earnest, for the final contest.

That second trial had awakened him to the danger of overconfidence, and in the third he was determined to take no risks. At the very stroke of the gong he raced up the steps as hard as he could, but his opponent's feet seemed to be winged. At the beginning of the second flight she passed him on her way down, her robe streaming behind her, so that he felt the wind it made; and near the top of the third flight she passed him on her second descent. Still, all he had now to do was to scramble through the trap-door on to the platform. But half-way through he stuck, and, though he struggled and twisted, his limbs seemed suddenly to have gone dead. She was still far below, but she had turned, and was once more coming up, approaching rapidly, with a sort of terrifying, screaming noise—not human, not even animal. Another effort brought him through the trap-door, all but one foot. He squirmed and wriggled over on to his stomach, he was nearly free, another twist would do it; and with that—at that last fateful moment—he felt just the tip of her long finger touch the sole of his shoe. He kicked out with his whole strength, but though he felt the full impact of his kick reach her, and she fell back and down and down, her finger still adhered to him, spinning out, thinner and thinner, longer and longer, like a spider's thread. There came a dull thud from below as her body reached the hall, and Tom struggled to his feet. But all was changed. It was blackest night, and he could see nothing. Roger, the very house itself, had disappeared; and the platform was shrunk to a single stone, upon which he stood poised dizzily above an infinite gulf. For two or three seconds he maintained his balance—horrible, agonizing seconds—then he crashed over and down. . . .

His own scream awakened him. He seemed to be in bed. . . . Yes, he was in bed, and now here was Mother; he heard her in the passage; and next moment his door was opened and she had turned on the light.

"Good morning," he said, managing a rather feeble little chuckle. "I suppose I disturbed you."

"It's all right," Mother answered quietly. "I hadn't gone to sleep or I shouldn't have heard you: you didn't waken Daddy."

"It was just a dream," he explained. "I dreamt I fell off a tower. You must have heard the flop."

Mother took no notice of this small joke, but she sat down beside his bed.

"Is it very late?" he asked.

"Not very. I don't really know. . . . I was reading. . . . Your prize, you see," and she held it up. "Would you like me to read to you for a little now?"

He signified assent, and turned over on his side, away from the light. Presently he shut his eyes; and when he opened them again it was morning, and down in the hall Mary was ringing the breakfast bell.

CHAPTER VIII

"Now boys, you've just ten minutes more, and then I shall collect the papers."

Tom, looking up at these words, encountered the passing glance of Miss Jimpson who had spoken them and who had presided over the examination from the beginning. Miss Jimpson smiled ever so little, therefore he immediately smiled back. She was nice-looking, he thought, and far younger than he had imagined schoolmistresses ever were: quite grown-up, of course, but not really much more than that: he hoped he would be in her class. That her name was Miss Jimpson he had learned when Mr. Pemberton, the headmaster, had come in a short while ago to see how they were all getting on.

There were fourteen other boys in the class-room besides himself, and their names had been called out in alphabetical order, though they were not now sitting in that order, Miss Jimpson having allowed them to choose their own seats. Tom knew none of them, but the majority appeared to know one another. From time to time he had scanned them with interest, wondering if he would like them. Macfarlane, the boy directly in front of him, had the appearance of an industrious and rather worried sheep. Macfarlane had begun to write from the very moment the papers had been handed round, and he had never stopped writing since. Tom himself had stopped only too frequently, but the whole experience was so new to him that he couldn't help watching the others. The boy beside him—Pascoe by name—was the most out-of-the-ordinary-looking. His sturdy body and tow-coloured hair were indeed ordinary enough; what made him look different was simply a very small, prim mouth, and the unusually wide space between two extremely serious blue eyes. Twice he had turned and caught Tom's speculative gaze fixed upon him, and the second time he had stared back with so severe an expression that the latter feared he must be offended. Thereupon a big boy seated some distance away, who had observed this brief and silent passage, winked, and then wrinkled up his nose in signal of the contempt and disgust with which Pascoe was to be regarded.

This boy, Brown, in spite of being the biggest boy there, evidently had exhausted all he had to say about the questions in the first half hour, which left him free, and obviously prepared to welcome any form of distraction. True, shortly before Miss Jimpson's warning that time was nearly up, he had had a further industrious period; but this had lasted only about five minutes, and from the movement of his hand, Tom suspected that art, not letters, was engaging him. Returning to his own labours, he had not written more than two or three lines when a tightly-rolled-up paper ball struck him on the nose before falling on the desk in front of him. The daring of this act nearly took Tom's breath away. Instinctively his first hasty glance was to see if Miss Jimpson had observed it, but Miss Jimpson was looking out of the window in absent-minded contemplation of her own private thoughts. Very stealthily, therefore, he unfolded the paper and smoothed it out, conscious all the time that Brown was watching him. It was, as he expected, a drawing—an extremely vulgar one too—representing, he supposed, the artist's impression of Pascoe. Not that it was in the least like him, but underneath it was scrawled: "The silly little fool next you"; and below that again, "What's *fierté*?"

"Pride," said Tom aloud, without thinking, and everybody looked up.

Miss Jimpson, recalled from her daydreams, spotted the speaker at once. "You mustn't talk, Barber," she told him, but not very sternly. "You did say something, didn't you?"

"I didn't mean to," Tom stammered, covered with confusion.

Miss Jimpson said no more, but several of the smaller boys looked slightly shocked. Not so Brown; who merely grinned broadly and gave him another wink, which Tom was much too shy to return.

The ten minutes having elapsed, Miss Jimpson now descended from the platform where she had been seated, and began to collect the papers. Everybody was ready for her with the exception of Macfarlane, who continued to write till she had practically to wrest his papers from him, and even then he seemed to relinquish them almost tearfully. "How could he have so much to say?" Tom marvelled. He *looked* stupid enough!

Anyhow, the exam was at an end, and Miss Jimpson, returning to her desk, with a few words dismissed them, saying they would meet again when school reopened, and that in the meantime she hoped they would all have very pleasant holidays.

Somebody, Tom felt, ought to have replied to this, but instead there was only the scuffle and noise of a hasty exodus, in which he joined, hanging a little behind the others. Out in the playground a general comparison of notes at once began. In this he was too shy to take part till Brown hailed him, gave him a playful poke in the ribs, and remarked genially, "Thanks for the tip, Skinny. . . . Not that it'll do much good."

Brown, in fact, appeared to take the examination very lightly indeed, and his own participation in it as being more in the nature of a joke than anything else. Quite soon he mounted his bicycle, and with a farewell, "See you in September, Skinny," rode away. The effect of his friendliness on the other hand remained; and though one tiresome result of it was that everybody thenceforth addressed him as Skinny, Tom found himself, so to speak, introduced and accepted.

Meanwhile, in the shrill babel of conflicting opinions, of confident assertions and flat contradictions, it was extremely difficult to judge how he had done in the examination. On the whole, he thought, pretty well, for the paper had suited him, being designed primarily as a test of general knowledge, whereas he had feared there might be a lot of arithmetic. One of the questions, for instance, had consisted simply in a list of five longish words, which you had to bring into five sentences of your own composition. He had enjoyed doing this, though like everybody else, except a red-haired boy called Preston, he had been floored by the word "frugality". Preston was the only one who had known what "frugality" meant—which just proves how much there is in luck, for *he* knew merely because there happened to be a picture called "The Frugal Meal" hanging above the mantelpiece in his dining-room at home. It was a Dutch picture, Preston said, and showed a Dutch family sitting down to a very skimpy-looking dinner. The sentence he had written was: "Since there was very little to begin with, and the parents each took two helpings, the children's meal was naturally one of great frugality."

This was considered pretty good, but Preston's cleverness was speedily forgotten in a general comment on the "squinty" behaviour of the parents, until it was discovered that actually there was nothing in the picture to justify the statement that they had taken two helpings. That was entirely due to Preston's own imagination. "Shows what you'll do when you've kids yourself," Haughton said, and everybody laughed.

Further ragging ensued, with the result that Preston, whose temper seemed uncertain, suddenly got mad. "How *could* it be in the picture?" he shouted, his face as red as his hair. "Lot of damned silly little fools! Here, give me back that paper, Skinny, or you'll get a punch in the jaw."

Skinny, who was no warrior, and as a matter of fact had been guilty of only one very mild witticism, hastily returned the paper, which Preston thrust angrily back into his pocket. A little later they all dispersed, singly or in groups, until only Pascoe was left. Pascoe, like most of the others, had a bicycle, but he walked beside Tom, wheeling it, and it was perfectly clear that he wanted to make friends. Tom himself felt no particular desire either one way or the other, but Pascoe was the only boy who had not called him Skinny, and moreover he now declared his intention of accompanying Tom part of the way home, which settled the matter. Pascoe, in fact, seemed very nice, though rather alarmingly serious, so that if you ventured on a joke you had subsequently to explain it to him, a task dreadfully calculated to reveal its true feebleness. Before long, nevertheless, several points in common were discovered; such as that neither possessed any brothers or sisters, that Pascoe thought an aquarium would be a jolly good scheme, and that, when Tom had finished with it, he would love to read *Curiosities of Natural History*. "I'm going to be a scientist, you see; very likely a naturalist. Only at Miss Wallace's, where I was at school till these hols., there was nobody to teach science. What are you going to be?"

Tom wasn't sure; he hadn't thought much about it; and changing the subject, he asked what Miss Wallace's had been like.

"Oh, all right," Pascoe replied half-heartedly; adding, after a pause: "Brown was there."

Somehow the tone in which this was uttered suggested that Brown was not among its happier memories, so Tom tactfully refrained from further questions, and it was Pascoe himself who proposed: "Couldn't we make the aquarium together? It would be better sport than doing it alone, and it could be at your place; I can easily ride over on my bike."

"I haven't a bike," Tom admitted, "so if you're sure you don't mind——"

"We'll need a net," Pascoe interrupted him. "I'll get Mother to make us one."

"So will I; we ought each to have one. . . . They'll need to be strong, too; so that the sticks won't bend when they're full of water. . . . When will you come?"

Pascoe considered. "I'll come to-morrow. Mother can make the net to-night."

This being arranged, he was on the point of turning back towards his own home, when Tom suddenly remembered he was going to Granny's to-morrow. It was a nuisance, for any other time would have done just as well, but it had been definitely settled. "I can't," he said, "I've got to go and stay for a week-end with Granny. But I'll be coming home on Monday."

"Well then——"

"Only I don't know what time; so it'd better be Tuesday."

"All right: I'll ride over first thing after breakfast, and I'll bring the net and a collecting-bottle. . . . Not if it's pouring rain, of course."

"Come anyway—if it's not too bad. There's heaps of things we can do inside. I've a sort of playroom up in the loft. And you needn't bother about bringing a bottle; Phemie has tons of glass jam-pots. . . . Besides, we'll have to fix up the aquarium itself first. I want to have it like a pond, and we'll need to dig a place for it."

"See you Tuesday then," Pascoe said, with one foot on the pedal. "And promise you won't begin to do anything till I come."

CHAPTER IX

Shortly after lunch, by arrangement, Doctor Macrory called to drive him to Tramore. Stretching out a large left hand, he opened the door of the front seat, and Tom, who had been waiting all ready in the porch, deposited a leather bag and Granny's book on the floor. He had just got in himself when Mother, evidently not expecting so rapid a departure, hastily emerged from the dining-room. "Well, I must say you're in a great hurry to be off! Am I not even to be allowed to say 'How do you do?' to Doctor Macrory? Granny ought to feel flattered. . . .

"It's extremely good of you to take him," she went on, coming to the window of the car; but the doctor said he had to visit a patient who lived in that direction anyhow, so no question of goodness was involved. "And I'll collect him for you some time on Monday afternoon," he added. "It'll probably be latish, but I don't suppose that matters."

"Of course it doesn't matter," Mother replied, "though there's nothing to prevent Edgar from collecting him, as you call it."

"Only that it would be several miles out of his way, and won't be out of mine: so you'd better tell him."

"If I do, may I tell him also that you'll be dining with us? You can, can't you?"

"Thus we see how infallibly virtue is rewarded," Doctor Macrory observed to Tom, as the car turned out on to the main road, and the latter leaned from the window to wave a last farewell. . . . "And now I want to hear all about yesterday's doings. To begin with, how did the examination go?"

"Very well, thank you," Tom replied.

Doctor Macrory chuckled. "That's good; but tell me a little more, won't you?—how it all struck you, what happened, and what the other boys were like."

Tom, at no time addicted to taciturnity, at once proceeded to do so. If it had been Daddy to whom he had been giving his account, it would have passed through a half-subconscious process of selection and elimination, based upon what he felt Daddy would or would not wish to hear, but with Doctor Macrory he never felt the need of this. So, as they drove between the summer fields, past farmsteads and an occasional wooded dingle, he gave him a minute description of everything and everybody, which he only broke off to utter a sudden "Oh!"—as the car swerved violently, the front mudguard narrowly missing a small child who had rushed out of a cottage in pursuit of a hen.

Doctor Macrory said "Damn!", and a moment later: "Did we get the hen?"—but Tom, gazing out behind, was able to assure him that both hen and child were safe.

"Well," said the doctor, "I'm afraid I interrupted you. You were telling me about the other boys. Brown I can't be sure of—there are so many Browns; but Preston, I fancy, is Bob Preston's son; and Pascoe quite certainly must be connected with the wine people—wholesale and retail—in Arthur Street. . . . In which case I was at school with his father."

"Do you get your wine from him?" Tom asked politely.

"I get my whisky from him," said Doctor Macrory, "so I suppose the answer is in the affirmative. . . . To return, however, to the main question—have any plans been made yet about what you're going to do at school? What subjects, I mean. Of course there'll be the usual subjects: what I really want to know is whether you're going to begin Greek. . . . You see," he went on, as Tom looked surprised, "I've been discussing that matter with your father, who doesn't quite share my views upon it. To me it is most important, but I'm not at all sure that my arguments convinced him; so a word from you yourself might not be out of place—in fact might settle things. What do you think?"

Tom had done a little, a very little Latin with Miss Sabine, but his classics ended there, and he didn't know what to think. In his uncertainty he suggested that there mightn't be anybody to *teach* Greek. At Miss Wallace's, for instance, where Pascoe had been, there hadn't been anybody to teach science; yet that was what Pascoe was most interested in, because he was going to *be* a scientist.

"Possibly he is," Doctor Macrory answered; "but unless I'm singularly mistaken you're not: Greek for you every time. . . . And of course there'll be somebody to teach it. . . . Science too, for that matter; though my own recollection of science at school is that it consisted largely in making fireworks and bad smells. . . . I really mean what I say, Tom, about learning Greek. I haven't met Master Pascoe, but the fact that you and he propose to make an aquarium together doesn't mean that science is at all likely to be in your line. You haven't that type of mind. If you're interested in natural history, it's only because, like the Greeks, you're fond of animals—which is a spiritual quality, and has nothing whatever to do with science."

Tom listened: he was in truth an excellent listener; as could be seen now from the thoughtful expression on his face. Doctor Macrory, noting that expression, may have wondered what he was thinking about, though he did not press him further.

It was indeed some little time before either of them spoke again, but at last, gazing out across the sunlit landscape, Tom said softly: "I'd like to learn Greek: I liked that book you lent me."

"Then you'd like their own writings still more. When you're a little older you must have a shot at your Uncle Stephen's book. There may be a good deal in it you won't understand, but you'll get something."

"I didn't know he had written a book," Tom said.

"Well, he has; and a good one."

Tom wondered why it had not been mentioned when Mother had told him other things about Uncle Stephen. Perhaps she didn't know about it, or had forgotten; but this seemed hardly likely. He pondered the singular lapse for some time before he asked: "Have we got it? Has Daddy got it?"

Doctor Macrory sounded his horn and slowed down to pass a flock of sheep. "I doubt it. It's not in your father's line; and unfortunately I don't possess a copy either."

"Is it in my line?" was Tom's next inquiry, for he found this matter of "lines" most interesting, though at the same time somewhat puzzling—puzzling to him, that was; Doctor Macrory appeared to find no difficulty.

The doctor smiled. "Very much, I should say; but not at present. It's a great mistake to read a book before you're ready for it. . . . I suppose you think I'm talking nonsense; but to start off with, you must remember that there's a bit of him in you—of your Uncle Stephen, I mean. Like dogs and other animals, we're all made up of bits of our ancestors, and his father was your great-grandfather, and his brother was your grandfather, and his niece is your mother."

Tom was impressed. "That makes a whole lot," he said, "not just a bit."

Doctor Macrory's glance again rested upon him, with an oddly reflective expression. It quite often did, Tom had noticed, proving that he was really interested and not just pretending to be; which was one reason why it was so much easier to talk freely to him than to Daddy.

"It does sound rather a lot—put in that way," the doctor admitted. "But the bits are discontinuous, you know; the only direct source is your great-grandfather."

"Is there anything about Orpheus in Uncle Stephen's book?" Tom asked after another pause. "In the book you lent me there was, but only a little."

"I'm afraid I don't remember: it's a good many years now since I read it. . . . I know there's a great deal about Hermes in it. Are you particularly interested in Orpheus?"

Tom hesitated. "It's just what it said about him in that book of yours—that when he played his music, all the animals and birds followed him and wanted to listen."

"And you'd like them to follow you?"

Tom laughed. "Of course I know it's only a story. Still, it *could* have happened, couldn't it? And there might be something about it in Uncle Stephen's book; because it says in your book that maybe it was Hermes who gave him his lyre."

"Does it? I'd forgotten that too. It's usually supposed to have been Apollo." He drove on for a while in silence. "I'm afraid I can't manage a lyre," he next said; "but since we're living in modern times, how would you like to experiment with a more modern instrument—the kind of pipe bird-charmers use, or used to use? I've a notion I've got one put away somewhere, if I can only lay my hands on it."

Tom coloured. "Do you mean——" he began, and abruptly stopped.

"Do I mean a present? Yes—that was the idea—if I can find it."

"But——"

"You won't be depriving me of anything. I've never used it in my life, and am never likely to. Whatever its effect on birds, I doubt if it would charm patients. It was merely given to me as a curiosity."

"Thanks most awfully——" Tom was beginning, when the doctor interrupted him. "And here we are! Do you think you can manage if I don't take you right up to the house? I'm rather behind time, I'm afraid; and if I go in I'll have to pay my respects to your grandmother, which will mean another five or ten minutes. That bag doesn't look very heavy."

CHAPTER X

Tom walked up an avenue over-arched by trees. It was not a particularly tidy avenue: indeed it badly required weeding at this moment, and he decided that he would perform that service for Granny to-morrow. With a hoe and a wheelbarrow it might be rather fun, and would at least help to pass the time, for to-morrow would be Sunday. If Mother were here she would certainly object on this very ground, but he had an idea that Granny's objections, if she had any, could be overcome. There was a saying employed by Phemie on such occasions, "The better the day the better the deed", and though really all it meant was that you intended to do what you wanted, it might work with Granny.

On the other hand, she probably didn't care a straw whether there were weeds in the avenue or not. Out of doors, she left everything to Nature, or what amounted to Nature, Quigley, who, with his wife, lived in the lodge, and was supposed to be her gardener. Both Mother and Daddy strongly disapproved of Quigley, and were always at Granny to get rid of him. They pointed out that he was lazy, incompetent, neglected his work, and imposed on her in every way he could. But of course Granny knew they had the irreproachable William in their mind's eyes, and to everything they said merely replied that she liked Quigley, and thought *he* liked *her*.

In fact, Granny had her own ideas, and was not easily influenced by other people's. Everything at Tramore was as different as possible from the garden at home. Granny didn't go in for flowers, therefore there were no flower-beds; and the only flowers were those which themselves wanted to be there; such as snowdrops, primroses, daffodils, and bluebells—all of them spring flowers and now over. Daddy didn't even approve of the Tramore grass, and again laid the blame on Quigley, because the sickle-shaped lawn in front of the house was thick with moss. William, he said, would have got rid of the moss long ago, but Quigley appeared to encourage it. Beyond the lawn, on every side, grew a green and tangled jungle. . . .

The house itself was covered thickly with creepers, so that looking at it from a little distance it appeared to sink into and be half lost in the leafy woodland behind. Granny preferred it like this, and so did Tom. In the late autumn and winter doubtless it presented a somewhat forsaken and neglected appearance, so that if it were not for the thin grey threads of smoke curling up from its irregular chimney-stacks, you might almost think nobody lived there; but on a summer afternoon, dreaming under a deep soft blue sky, it had a rich and drowsy beauty, profoundly peaceful. . . .

And here, like Mariana in her moated grange, lived Granny. Tom had learned the poem about Mariana for Miss Sabine, and, as with most of the poems he was fondest of, had found its counterpart in real life. Naturally it was only the "moated grange" itself which was a counterpart, for Mariana had been young and most unhappy, whereas Granny was old and remarkably lively: still, the picture and the music were the same——

All day within the dreamy house,
The doors upon their hinges creak'd,
The blue fly sung in the pane; the mouse
Behind the mouldering wainscot shriek'd,
Or from the crevice peer'd about.
Old faces glimmer'd thro' the doors,
Old footsteps trod the upper floors,
Old voices called her from without.

It was lovely. Daddy, to be sure, had said that Miss Sabine's taste in poetry seemed to be very nearly as morbid as Tom's own—when *he* was a boy, he had been given such things as "Ye Mariners of England", and "How they Brought the Good News from Ghent to Aix", to learn. This had made Mother laugh. "But you didn't enjoy them very much, dear, did you?—though they *were* so stirring; and Tom at least likes his." And since Daddy returned no answer: "I think it's wonderful how Miss Sabine always knows what he *will* like. It's very clever of her, and certainly makes his lessons much easier and pleasanter."

"Oh, they're a nice pair!" Daddy had grumbled; but Tom knew he really thought a tremendous lot of Miss Sabine.

The outer door of the house was open, so he did not need to ring the bell. He turned the handle of the inner door and entered the hall, which was square and had a fireplace in it, making it look like a room. Here he left down his bag, and went in search of Granny. He knew where she always sat; and there he found her—in the big panelled drawing-room, with its bright chintzes and soft grey carpet, and the cabinets where she kept her collection of china. Granny herself, sitting so quietly among her things, was not unlike some delicate and fragile object surviving from an earlier period. She looked, somehow, as if nothing had ever happened to her. Her tranquil, gentle face, with its faint wild-rose colouring; her white hair; her slender hands; even her knitting—were all singularly in keeping with the porcelain cups and plates and vases she was so fond of. A fantastic notion crossed Tom's mind that Granny was growing more and more to resemble her things. The yellow sunlight, filtering through curtained windows, awoke the dragons on a Chinese screen behind her to a fiery life; the whole room was flooded with magic light and colour; a single silvery note from a small clock on the chimney-piece chimed the half-hour.

But Granny—who could not have heard his arrival or she would have been out in the hall to meet him—at once became very human indeed, as she got up quickly from her chair to kiss him welcome. "Tom darling, it's so nice of you to have come. Does Rose know you're here? Perhaps you'd better touch the bell. I wasn't quite sure when you would arrive."

Granny was always a little extravagant in her endearments, as indeed, according to Mother, in everything else; but when there was nobody there Tom didn't mind this; and at all events she didn't bother you about such matters as going to bed on the first stroke of the clock, or keeping your hands in your pockets, or eating between meals—in fact she would have fed him from morning till night if she had had her way.

He produced his parcel. Here's your book, Granny: Mother got it in town; and there's a lovely tiger in it."

"Thank you very much, dear. Doctor Macrory brought you, I suppose. Your mother rang me up last night to tell me he was going to."

"Yes; but he only came as far as the gate. . . . Where's Dinah?"

"Dinah is in the kitchen with her kittens. Perhaps you didn't know she'd had kittens?"

Tom was immediately interested. "Why don't you have them in here?" he asked.

"It's too soon yet: their eyes aren't even open. Rose says they're just like little rats. But the next time you come——"

Tom interrupted her. "Do you mean to say you haven't even *looked* at them, Granny? Kittens aren't a bit like rats. They've got fur, and whiskers, and everything. Rats are naked when they're born."

"Well, that's what Rose says," Granny answered meekly; and as the door opened, "Oh Rose, I did ring for tea, but perhaps you wouldn't mind bringing in Dinah's basket: Master Tom wants to see the kittens."

"I'll get it myself," Tom cried, jumping up. "How many are there, Rose?"

"I'm sure I never counted them," Rose replied with an air of superiority. "Nasty crawling little things! Cook says there *were* five; but she gave three of them to Quigley to be drowned."

Tom regarded her coldly. He did not approve of affectation, especially of Rose's kind—just as if kittens were far beneath her. "Then if there were five, and three have been drowned, you ought to be able to tell how many are left," he said.

He knew this wasn't a proper way to speak, and Rose, maintaining a lofty silence, evidently thought so too. All the same, it was what she deserved, so he left her there, and ran out to the kitchen to get the basket.

Dinah was in it with her children, but Dinah, too, behaved stupidly. The moment he lifted the basket she hopped out, with a distinctly irritated mew. She very soon altered her tone, however, to a more humble and plaintive one, as he carried the basket back to the other room, while she followed closely on his heels. This anxiety was extremely silly, and he told her so. If *he* couldn't be trusted with kittens, he would like to know who could! "Nobody," poor Dinah replied; and since she had already lost three, her pessimism was perhaps excusable.

Not that she appeared to suspect him of wishing to steal the kittens; from the tone of her mews it was more as if she feared he might break them by letting them drop; and she got back into the basket the moment it was deposited on the hearthrug. She didn't remain there long. Tom took the whole family out and lay down on the hearthrug himself, curling as well as he could round both cat and kittens till all felt warm and furry—and very soon purry, too; with a rough tongue, intended for a kitten, occasionally passing over the back of his hand.

From these domestic felicities he was summoned by Granny to come to the table and have tea. At home there would have been a reminder to go and wash his hands first, and Granny received due credit for being sensible and unfussy. She got yet a further good mark for having remembered that he was specially fond of potted shrimps and hot freshly-baked shortbread. Dinah, though unused to any but kitchen meals, also was comforted with a few shrimps, and a saucer of milk—a good deal of which she splashed on to the carpet.

"Granny, have you got Uncle Stephen's book?"

Granny, who had been beaming benevolently at nothing in particular—merely in a sort of general amiability—shook her head. She seemed not even to have grasped the importance of the question, for she went on pressing food upon him as if he were never to expect another meal.

"But Granny, you *must* have. Grandpapa was Uncle Stephen's brother, you know."

Granny, continuing to beam, again shook her head.

"Do you mean to say he *wasn't* his brother!" Tom cried, both incredulous and indignant.

At this Granny pulled herself together. "No, dear, of course he was his brother; but your Uncle Stephen was ten years younger than Grandpapa, and for a long time lived abroad. Then, when he came back to this country, he shut himself up at Kilbarron, where he has lived ever since. Grandpapa *did* write once, asking him to pay us a visit, but we never even got a reply—so naturally that ended the matter."

"Why don't *you* write, Granny?"

Granny laughed. "Perhaps I shall. And tell him he's got a nephew who's most anxious to meet him."

Tom pondered a moment. "Will you write to-night, Granny?"

But Granny had either exhausted or been exhausted by the subject. "Is this your mother?" she asked, "or is it Doctor Macrory? It must be either one or the other."

"It was Doctor Macrory," Tom admitted, "but Mother told me about him too. She thinks I take after him."

Granny seemed amused. "Since she never set eyes on him in her life, that at least does credit to her powers of imagination; but I should have thought Doctor Macrory would have had more sense."

Tom was disappointed, though at the same time not convinced. After all, he had much more faith in Mother's judgement than in Granny's, while Doctor Macrory was by far the most sensible person he had ever met. For a minute or two he remained silent, and then he asked; "Would you mind if I went all over the house, Granny?"

Granny, if she appeared to be slightly puzzled by this abrupt digression, at least had no objections. "Of course, dear, you can go over the house. Why not?"

But the very promptness of her agreement made Tom doubt whether she had understood what he meant. "I mean now," he explained. "I mean the locked-up rooms in the east wing. I've never been up there except once, when there was a spring-cleaning."

At this a sudden light dawned, and Granny looked slightly annoyed. "If you're still thinking of that book," she declared, "I *know* it isn't there. Why are you so unbelieving? There are no books there except a lot of rubbish—old school-books and magazines, and perhaps a few yellow-backs."

"Yes, Granny; but do you mind if I go up?"

"Whether I mind or not," Granny told him, "I think you're an extremely persistent little boy, and I hoped you had come to see me."

Tom sighed. "So I have, Granny. . . . I'll be seeing you all this evening, and to-morrow, and part of Monday. We can play backgammon after dinner—or even draughts."

The "even", though entirely unpremeditated, was not lost upon Granny, who could not help recollecting that draughts had figured not infrequently as an entertainment on similar occasions in the past. He was certainly a very odd little boy, but she was much too old and too fond of him to be offended for more than a moment. "Run along," she said, "since you're so bent on it. . . . Tell Rose to give you the key of the door at the top of the stairs: all the other doors are unlocked."

CHAPTER XI

Tom did as she told him, though he would have felt more comfortable if she hadn't made those remarks about his persistence. After all, Granny *did* forget things; he had often heard her say she would be forgetting her own name next; and simply because he wished to make quite sure didn't mean that he was unbelieving. Very likely she hadn't been up in the empty rooms for ages, and even if she had, she wouldn't have been looking for Uncle Stephen's book. In fact she didn't seem to take the least interest in either Uncle Stephen *or* his book. That it wasn't downstairs, Tom himself was certain, for there were only two bookcases downstairs and he had gone over their contents heaps of times. Nor had it taken long: Tramore wasn't a booky house: Daddy had ten times as many. . . .

The staircase rose from the hall, first in a single broad flight with very wide shallow treads, and then branching to right and left in two narrower flights terminating in and connected by a railed gallery. The closed rooms were in the east wing—the old nursery quarters, Granny said—and the locked door through which you reached them was at one end of this gallery. It was a queer arrangement, Tom thought, but there were unnecessary doors all over Granny's house, just as if everybody had wanted to live as separately as they could from everybody else; and of course, if it were kept open, you mightn't notice the door. He opened it now, and after a moment's hesitation shut it behind him. It was lighter here than it had been in the hall or on the stairs, because the doors of all the rooms were wide open and their windows unblinded. Not that there were really many rooms—only four, and one of them was a bathroom. It was in the biggest—perhaps the old nursery—that he found the books, and a single glance told him that Granny had been right about them. They were arranged on a couple of hanging shelves and were just such a worn-out, tattered collection as you might find in the fourpenny box outside any second-hand bookseller's. She had even overrated them, for there were only three yellow-backs, the rest were railway-guides, hymn-books, spelling-books, geographies and grammars, with some bound volumes of magazines. Granny certainly would be able to say, "I told you so," or "Perhaps you'll believe me next time." At least that was what most people would have said.

The inference, indeed, was plain—Uncle Stephen hadn't given Grandpapa his book, and Grandpapa hadn't bought it. For that matter, nobody seemed to have bought it—not even Doctor Macrory—and Tom felt more in sympathy with Uncle Stephen than ever.

He went over to the window and looked out. From up here you got a much better view than from the rooms downstairs, and he opened the window and leaned over the sill. Beyond the lawn, the ground took a slight dip downward, and then rose again to the skyline. It would be a splendid place for animals, he decided. You could have all kinds of animals here, and Granny hadn't even a dog—nobody but Dinah and her two kittens. He began to make plans of what he would do if he were Granny. First, he would build a very high wall all round, so that there could be really wild animals, like those they have in zoos. Next, the dogs would have to be taught not to chase anything—which would be easy enough with Roger and Barker. He would have snakes, too, in spite of Saint Patrick. Only with so many animals to take care of he would need somebody to help him, and as Quigley would be no good he would get James-Arthur from Denny's. . . .

Tom could not have told what it was that at this point made him suddenly look round. He had heard no sound of footsteps—consciously he had heard no sound at all—nevertheless, standing in the passage just outside the door, was a boy watching him—a boy of about his own age, or perhaps younger, dressed in a dark blue jersey and shorts. He was standing in the full sunlight, and possibly had been there for some time, though the moment Tom looked round he hastily retreated and was gone. Tom himself was so taken aback that for a minute or two he simply stared at the empty doorway without moving. Who was he? Either Cook or Rose must have sent him up; and probably it was Cook, for he knew she had nephews, though he had never seen them. It was pretty cheeky of him all the same—to steal up on tip-toe like this, and then run away. . . . Unless he had suddenly turned shy. . . . And perhaps he hadn't run away; perhaps he was only hiding, in a kind of game. To make sure, Tom crossed to the door and peeped out. Yes—he was there—but now he was in the doorway at the end of the passage, and as before, the moment Tom caught a glimpse of him he disappeared. . . .

It evidently *was* a game, yet Tom felt half annoyed as well as puzzled. "If he imagines I'm going to run after him, he's very much mistaken," he said to himself. "He can either go or stay as he pleases."

Then, while he stood there, uncertain what to do next, he began to think. . . . If this had been Cook's nephew, wouldn't Cook herself have come up to explain, to perform some kind of introduction? Besides, he somehow didn't look like Cook's nephew—or at least what Tom would have expected Cook's nephew to look like. . . . Did Granny know any boys? If she did, he had never heard of them; and anyhow, she, too, would either have come up with the visitor or have called Tom down. It certainly was very queer; the boy's behaviour even more so. . . .

There he was again—he had come back—but this time he lingered, perhaps because Tom had not followed him. He was not in the sunlight now, yet surely there was a light, a kind of brightness, that seemed to be in the air behind him and all round him. A sudden memory was stirred in Tom's mind. He knew neither how nor whence it had come, but it was there, and held him hushed and spellbound. That other boy—Ralph Seaford—this was where he once had lived—this was his home—

Tramore. With nearly the whole length of the passage between them, Tom remained motionless—hardly startled—not really frightened at all, for the boy was smiling at him, half timidly, half doubtfully, yet as if he wanted very much to make friends. There was an interval before Tom smiled back, but in the end he did, seeing which the boy's smile instantly deepened, and step by step he drew nearer, coming very slowly down the passage.

"I know who you are," Tom said, hardly above his breath. "At least I think I do."

There was no answer, and, though the boy was close beside him now, Tom somehow knew that if he stretched out his hand it would touch nothing, that he was near and yet not near, there and yet not there.

Side by side they returned to the room where the books were. No sound passed the boy's lips, nevertheless Tom was as sure as if he had said so that he wanted to be with him, to play with him, that this was why he had come. Somehow the thought was oddly pathetic, and awoke an immediate response. Only what could they play at? If they had been at home it would have been easy enough; he could have set his railway going—which he rarely did for himself—he could have shown his yacht, or built a house with his bricks: but here there was nothing except a lot of dusty antiquated furniture and household odds and ends—boxes and trunks, either empty or packed with old clothes, old bills, old letters—for Granny seemed never to destroy anything.

Presently his glance fell on a pile of ancient *Graphics* on the floor by the window. These might at least be better than nothing. So lifting an armful on to the table he sat down and began to turn the leaves, pausing at the full-page pictures, while the boy leaned forward to look too, his hand seeming to rest on Tom's shoulder although Tom could feel no pressure there.

Tom talked about the pictures, because it was easier to talk aloud. Yet he had no idea whether his companion could hear him, or simply understood him without words. The sense of communication at any rate was there—vividly there; and by and by even the feeling of strangeness was lost. The sunlight slanted across the room; and the rustle of leaves, and the gay careless music of birds, floated in through the open window. Now and then Tom glanced at the face that was so close to his, and always, when he did so, it broke into a smile—happy and strangely trusting. . . .

Time slipped by unnoticed; the shadows outside were lengthening. At last, breaking in upon them unexpectedly, came the deep and distant notes of the hall gong. It was meant for him, Tom knew, a reminder that he must get ready for dinner; and he also knew that if he neglected the summons a very cross Rose would soon appear to fetch him. "I must go," he whispered, yet with a feeling of compunction. He really did feel distressed, for the small figure beside him looked infinitely forlorn and lonely the moment he had spoken the words. But he had understood, and he stepped back at once. "I can't help it," Tom went on: "I'll come again if I possibly can; though I know Granny will think it very queer and ask questions, and, and—— Goodbye." Deliberately he averted his eyes, and without another look or word ran out of the room and along the passage and down the stairs. . . .

At dinner, Granny had an unusually quiet guest beside her. Before long she noticed it. "What are you dreaming about?" she asked, half amused, and half curious. "I suppose you'll say 'nothing', but you might at least tell me what you found upstairs to keep you there for two hours. I very nearly sent Rose up to see. It can't have been the books."

"No," Tom answered, in a rather subdued voice. Actually he had forgotten all about the books.

"Granny——" he began presently, and stopped, leaving her to wait expectantly while he stared at the opposite wall.

Granny, however, was not unaccustomed to such pauses, and allowed him to take his own time. He did, and in the end decided it would be better not to say what he had been going to say. Instead, he told her that he had liked it upstairs, and had been looking at pictures in the *Graphic*. "I didn't finish them," he added, so that he might have an excuse for a second visit.

Unfortunately Granny, in her innocence, at once upset this stratagem by replying that she would tell Rose to bring them down to the drawing-room after dinner.

CHAPTER XII

Late on Monday afternoon, Doctor Macrory "collected" him as he had promised, and they drove home together. On the way, the doctor told him he had been unable to find the bird-call, adding that he now didn't think it would have been of much use even if he had—was not, that is to say, the kind of thing Tom wanted. "At any rate, I consulted a friend of mine who's a great bird man, and he said the only instruments of the sort he had ever seen were of German manufacture and purely mechanical—each one separately designed to reproduce the mating call of a different bird. There wouldn't be much fun in that, would there? and I expect mine must be the same. What *you* want is something on which you can play—if not like Orpheus, at least like the shepherds in Theocritus—something more in the nature of Pan-pipes; and I imagine the nearest modern instrument to that is a mouth-organ, so I got you one. . . . It's there," he went on, nodding towards the shelf in front of Tom's seat, upon which lay a small parcel wrapped up in brown paper.

Tom opened it, a little disappointed, but only momentarily, for after all he had never possessed a mouth-organ. "Thanks most awfully," he said; and from time to time during the remainder of the drive he blew a note or two, though very softly, in case these experimental sounds should not be pleasing to the doctor.

No one was in sight when the car turned in at the gate, but they had not arrived many minutes—in fact he had only had time to go into the house and be kissed by Mother and come out again—when Roger appeared. Roger had missed him a lot, it seemed. At least twice every day, Mother said, he had come over from the farm in search of his friend, and had looked so disappointed at not finding him that she herself had gone out to talk to him, because she thought he deserved it for being so faithful. Tom thought so too, and their first greetings over, sat down on the lawn to pet him. It was strange that dogs should be so much more trustful and easily made happy than human beings. Roger demanded no explanations or apologies; he simply turned over on to his back, waving his four legs absurdly in the air, pretending to be a puppy. Tom rubbed his chest and tumbled him over, now on this side and now on that, while Roger growled and bit and rolled his eyes, which was all part of the puppy game; and when the sound of the gong interrupted them, he followed Tom into the cloak-room, where he sat watching him while he washed his hands. After that he would have gone out as usual to wait on the lawn had not Tom given him a whispered signal from the dining-room door.

This was a "try-on", as James-Arthur would have said, and Daddy immediately spotted it. "Go out, sir!" he commanded sternly, and Roger, with drooping head and tail was turning to obey, when Mother—melted it may be by his air of dejection—came to the rescue. "Oh well, perhaps for once!" she murmured, and clever old Roger, needing no more, instantly stretched himself beside Tom's chair. Here, knowing he was only there on sufferance, he kept so still that all might have been well, and his presence very soon forgotten, had not Tom surreptitiously given him a spoonful of soup. Roger accepted it, but with so resounding a thump of his tail on the floor that naturally it attracted the attention of Daddy, who this time rose ominously from the table.

"Come on, sir; out you go!"—and before anybody could utter a word of protest, poor Roger was hustled from the room, and the door shut with what was very like a bang.

"Disgusting!" Daddy continued, returning to his seat. "Feeding him with the same spoon you're using yourself!"

Doctor Macrory smiled one of his barely perceptible smiles, while Mother looked reproachfully at the offender as much as to say, "Now you've put *me* in the wrong!" And to relieve the situation she went on aloud; "You haven't told us yet how you got on at Granny's. Did you give her her book?"

Tom glanced furtively at Daddy, but Daddy's countenance had not relaxed. "Yes," he replied; and after a pause: "Some of Granny's other pictures are like that—like the pictures in the book."

As it chanced, he could not have hit on a more fortunate remark, for it straightway turned the conversation to Granny's collections of Oriental prints and china, which Doctor Macrory declared he envied her. Granny, he said, must have a wonderful flair, and not only that, but have been uncommonly lucky as well.

"As a matter of fact, it was really Father who collected them," Mother said, "and at a time when such things were much easier to find and much less expensive than they are to-day."

"But Granny helped him," Tom put in loyally: "she told me she did."

"For my part," Mother went on, ignoring Granny's advocate, "though the china is very nice, I must say I prefer European pictures"—which led to an animated discussion between her and Doctor Macrory as to whether it is possible to appreciate pictures of completely different kinds even supposing they are equally good.

The doctor thought not, "for the simple reason that for us as individuals they never *can* be equally good. I remember visiting an exhibition of early Dutch masters and trying my hardest to wax enthusiastic over a picture of a hare by Jan Weenix—supposed to be the gem of the collection. Which, in a way, I dare say it was. Only all the time I couldn't help wondering why he should have wanted to paint a dead hare hanging up by its feet when he might just as easily have painted a living one. . . . It was the same with several of the other pictures; the painting was marvellous, but the subject appeared to be a matter of indifference—whether it was a madonna or a child with diarrhoea."

Daddy, who on principle never agreed with Doctor Macrory, here found a few words to say in favour of the child with diarrhoea. It struck Tom as a rather strange topic to choose at dinner-time, but the argument was academic, and as it proceeded became more and more metaphysical, and less and less comprehensible so far as he was concerned. It was the kind of argument, however, both Daddy and Doctor Macrory loved, and it lasted so long that dinner was practically over when Phemie, very red in the face, abruptly terminated it by bursting into the room.

"If you please, ma'am, will you come and speak to Mary. I can't do anything with her, and she's going on the way you never heard the like—crying and sobbing about a ghost she says is upstairs."

"A ghost!" Mother repeated feebly, staring at Phemie in bewilderment. "What kind of ghost?"

At this both Daddy and Doctor Macrory laughed, but Phemie was nearly choking with bottled-up indignation. "You may well ask!" she cried, "and it's what I asked myself, for it might be a whole regiment of them from the noise she's making. But sure it's only the ghost of a little boy, up in Master Tom's room. . . . She says she won't sleep another night in the house, and——"

Mother rose with a sigh and followed Phemie to the kitchen, while Daddy observed, "One of the lesser domestic felicities which you, Doctor, as a bachelor, I presume have to forgo." Then, with a twinkle in his eye, he turned to his son: "You must have brought the ghost with you, Tom, from Granny's."

It was an ill-timed joke if ever there was one, and Tom tried vainly to hide his discomposure. Little did Daddy know how true his words were, or he might not have spoken them so lightly! With a mumbled apology he rose abruptly from the table, but Daddy immediately asked; "Where are you going to?"

He hesitated guiltily, avoiding the two pairs of eyes he now felt to be fixed upon him. At last he stammered: "I'm going upstairs to—to look."

"Sit down," Daddy told him quietly, "and don't be silly. She probably saw a curtain flapping, or something equally terrifying"—and he actually cracked a walnut and pushed the decanter in the direction of Doctor Macrory, who appeared to be equally unperturbed.

Tom sat down, but it was only with the greatest effort that he remained seated. The possibility of any such development as this had never crossed his mind. He had found no opportunity before leaving Granny's to pay a further visit to the closed rooms: or rather, there had no longer *been* any closed rooms; for the very next day Granny herself had gone up to inspect them, with the result that she had suddenly taken it into her head to have them tidied up, cleaned out, the floors scrubbed, and even the woodwork touched up with fresh paint, so that from then on either Quigley or Mrs. Quigley had been in constant possession. This, so far as ghosts were concerned, had effectually ended the adventure; and pondering on it quietly and at leisure Tom had even come to be half persuaded that it was his own private adventure—by which he meant that other people, had they been there, would have seen nothing. . . .

Yet now Mary had seen. . . . Only, why Mary . . . ? And why, above all, here at home—miles away from Tramore . . . ? And *what* had she seen?

Meanwhile Doctor Macrory and Daddy had once more taken up their interrupted discussion, but they broke it off the moment Mother returned, and all three looked at her, Tom with round anxious eyes, the other two in a sort of amused inquiry. Mother herself was less amused than vexed, though she veered oddly between the two as she recounted what had taken place. It appeared that she and Phemie had managed between them either to cajole or bully the unfortunate Mary into a more reasonable, or at any rate a more submissive frame of mind. Mother had taken the line that there was no ghost, that it was all nonsense; Phemie, accepting the ghost, had dwelt scornfully on its diminutive size. "It's asking the mistress's forgiveness you ought to be, Mary Donaghy, instead of roaring and rampaging round the house, the way it might be Doctor Crippen or some of them ones was after you!"

Tom did not smile. Phemie may or may not have used those

words, but Mother only repeated them because she thought they were funny. Her own description of poor Mary was very far from bearing them out. "There she sat, the tears streaming down her face, though if I told her once I told her fifty times, 'There are no such things as ghosts.'"

"That surely was a rather rash statement," Doctor Macrory observed. "According to the great Milton, 'millions of spiritual creatures walk the earth unseen, both when we wake and when we sleep'."

"Yes, unseen," Mother retorted, and Daddy asked curiously: "What actually does she say she *did* see?"

"Oh, she now admits she only *thought* she saw something—a little boy—standing by the window—and he was gone next moment. . . . It's a pity he *did* go, for it's chiefly that which seems to have frightened her."

But at this point Tom ceased to listen. The preoccupation of the others gave him the opportunity he had been waiting for, and slipping quietly away, he ran upstairs to his own room. He opened the door precipitately, but whatever he may have expected to find he did not find; the room was empty, and empty it remained, though he waited on for some time.

He did not know whether this was a good sign or the reverse, but at least there was nothing he could do about it. Perhaps the trouble was over and might not happen again; and since he could not stay up here indefinitely, and did not want to rejoin the others, who would still be talking about it, he decided that he might as well go down to the kitchen and get some bread-and-milk for his hedgehog.

There, however, the sight of Mary renewed his uneasiness, mingled now with a sense of irritation. For she was seated in a chair in a lax and mournful fashion, very much as Mother had described her, suggesting something between a sagging bolster and Watts's picture of the abandoned Ariadne. Even if she *had* seen Ralph, Tom thought impatiently, what was there to make such a fuss about? and he cast a sidelong and unsympathetic glance at her. Phemie, too, every time she looked in Mary's direction, emitted a disdainful sniff.

Leaving them to settle their own troubles, Tom went out into the garden and down to the hedge at the foot of it. Roger must either have grown tired of waiting or been offended by Daddy's treatment of him, for he had gone home. Everybody, Tom thought, seemed to be at cross-purposes and at variance with everybody else, and it was all most stupid.

He sat down under the bank, close to a deserted rabbit-hole, and gave a low call, which he repeated at intervals until Alfred peeped out. Then his mood instantly changed, and his misgivings were forgotten. Alfred had brought a friend with him to-night—either that, or he had acquired a wife. At any rate they both shared the bread-and-milk—Alfred boldly and confidently—the wife, if she *was* his wife, at first timidly. They had odd little faces, with tiny black eyes, small ears, and long, sensitive noses; and in spite of their very short legs they could climb up and down the bank and across Tom with surprising agility. He hoped they would soon have a family, for he had never seen very young hedgehogs, and they must be dear little things. Alfred had only come to live in the rabbit-hole that spring, or at any rate had only been discovered then, and by the stupid William of all people, who had found him on the croquet-lawn, half-way through a hoop, and been frightened to touch him. Luckily Tom had not been far off at the time, and had lifted him out of danger in spite of William's warning that his spikes were poisonous. William had wanted to kill him with his spade, which was just like William. He insisted that hedgehogs ought to be destroyed, that they devoured eggs and young birds, and carried away apples on their spines, though this last was so obviously untrue that you wouldn't have thought even he could have believed it. Daddy, fortunately, soon put a stop to that nonsense, and told him they were the most useful things you could have in a garden, and got rid of far more slugs than any of William's own contrivances. At which William had moved off, muttering to himself, and of course still firmly convinced that he knew better. . . .

"Tom! Tom!" It was Mother calling to him—to go to bed, he supposed. He didn't want to go to bed, but since Alfred and his wife had now finished the bread-and-milk he lifted the empty dish and returned slowly to the house.

Mother was waiting for him on the lawn, and half involuntarily, while he walked beside her, he asked the question he had very nearly asked Granny. His mind, indeed, was at present so full of it, that he asked it just as if they had already been discussing the matter. "Suppose there was a boy who wanted very much to play with another boy, *could* he come back? I mean—I mean, do you believe he could?"

It was only after he had uttered the words, and seen Mother's purposely blank expression, that he realized they had *not* been talking. "I'm afraid I don't understand," she said. "Could who come back? And come back from where?"

"I don't know," Tom answered doubtfully. "From—from heaven, perhaps."

Mother, after studying his face for a moment, abandoned subterfuge. "This, I suppose, is Mary's work! Phemie's also, for she at any rate ought to have known better. I was extremely angry with both of them."

"But how was it Phemie's fault?" Tom expostulated. "How could she help about Mary?"

"She could help bursting into the room the way she did—before Doctor Macrory too. What was to prevent her from calling me out and speaking to me in private? Only they never consider anybody but themselves. And as for Mary! I could have smacked her—great stupid lump—sitting there moaning and groaning over nothing! Probably some trash she'd been reading—about ghosts and murders and——"

"Mary reads love stories," Tom thought it only fair to point out.

"Well, it's the same thing," Mother rather wonderfully replied: "never anything sensible. . . . Now, I suppose, we'll be treated to a similar scene every time she has to go upstairs by herself in the dark."

"It wasn't dark," Tom again pointed out. "And," he added, "if you're thinking of me you needn't worry, for I don't care a straw."

His words, or more perhaps the tone in which they were

uttered, must have had the right effect, for Mother, while seeming slightly surprised, also appeared considerably relieved. She gave him a long look, and then suddenly smiled. "No—I don't believe you do," she declared. "Well, I'm glad you're such a sensible boy. . . . People of that class are always superstitious—terrified if they hear a death-watch beetle, or break a looking-glass, or dream of a hearse."

This at least cleared the air for the time being: nevertheless, later on, and up in his own room, Tom half wished Ralph *would* come, if only that he might be warned of all the trouble he had made. And just before he fell asleep he fancied he *did* see him, but in a half-dream, between sleeping and waking. "You must stay in Granny's house," he whispered very gently—"in your own house—or go back to—to wherever you really come from. . . . I'm sorry, but you can see for yourself what happens when you don't. It would be all right if there was only me, but I think other people—*some* other people—like Mary—can see you too—and they're frightened. They can't help it, I expect. . . . They don't understand. . . . Do, please, go back."

CHAPTER XIII

Tom, Roger, Barker, and Pincher were all in the garden next morning when Pascoe, armed with a fishing-net and waders, arrived. As his approach was heralded by a good deal of ringing of his bicycle-bell, naturally the three dogs, unaccustomed to such spectacular entrances, hastened to assist him to dismount; which he did precipitately, eliciting a cry of anguish from Barker, upon whose paw he had descended, and yelps of delight from the excitable Pincher, who had grabbed him by the jacket.

"I say—call your beastly dogs off, can't you!" Pascoe shouted, for Pincher, relinquishing the jacket, had now got hold of the handle of the fishing-net, and in the tug-of-war that followed, the bicycle clattered to the ground.

"What are you laughing at?" Pascoe screamed. "If he gets the net he'll tear it to pieces! Let go, dash you!" But Tom had already caught Pincher by the scruff of the neck, and a monitory smack brought him to order.

"It's your own fault," he said, "for kicking up such a row. If you'd come in quietly like anybody else it wouldn't have happened. . . . Anyhow, they're not my dogs; they're only friends."

Pascoe, however, had already recovered his natural calm, and was now studying the canine bodyguard with a thoughtful expression. He seemed to be pondering something, with the result that presently he turned his gaze upon Tom himself, and pronounced solemnly: "If I were you I'd keep them here for a while."

"Keep them?" Tom echoed, bewildered by this sudden change. "Do you mean all the time? How can I keep them when they're not mine?"

"You could borrow them," Pascoe replied, "and I'll tell you why. I was going to warn you in any case, so that you could let your people know."

A pause ensued, which was broken in the end rather impatiently by Tom. "Well—why *don't* you warn me? Is it something you're too scared even to mention?"

"No it isn't," Pascoe retorted, "and I've a good mind now not to tell you."

"You needn't if you don't want to: I don't care."

Since this was obviously untrue, Pascoe took no notice of it. "It's a man," he said slowly. "He's hanging about outside, and he was staring in through your gate when I came along. He didn't know I was watching him, but I was. . . . Because I guessed from the way he was behaving what he was really up to. . . . He was reconnoitring."

"Reconnoitring?" Tom was becoming more and more mystified. He could see that the word was intended to be impressive, and he knew what it meant of course; but he associated it with military tactics, which didn't seem to make sense here.

"They always do," Pascoe went on darkly, "before they break into a house. It's to get the exact position of everything fixed in their minds, so that they won't make a mistake if there's an alarm and they have to make a sudden bolt for it."

Tom was now gazing at him open-mouthed, which appeared to afford Pascoe a gloomy satisfaction. "You mean he was a burglar? But how could you possibly tell?"

"Because he was in disguise," Pascoe answered. "He was disguised as a tramp."

This, somehow, was a little *too* much, and Tom recovered his equanimity. He was extremely curious, nevertheless, and wanted to learn more, so he only said: "He must have known you were there."

"Naturally, in the end, he did; seeing that I got off my bicycle and spoke to him."

"You——" There flashed across Tom's mind a picture of Pascoe's attitude when Brown had approached him in the playground, and Brown was a good deal less formidable than a burglar. The corners of his mouth twitched, but he repressed a temptation to laugh. "What did you say?"

"I asked him if he knew where you lived. I had to have some excuse, so that he wouldn't suspect I had penetrated his disguise."

"And *did* he know where I lived?"

"He *said* he didn't, but he gave me a very queer look, and then began to tell me a lot of lies—that he was out of work and just looking round in the hope of getting some kind of job, such as clipping hedges or sawing wood; that his wife was sick, and that they had five children and were expecting a sixth; and that the eldest was a boy about my age and very like me in appearance, though of course not so good-looking."

"Why 'of course'?" Tom asked.

"Well, I'm only telling you what he said," Pascoe returned huffily. "If you don't want to hear I can stop. . . . Later on, he said something about his *six* children, and it was then I saw it had been all lies."

"I don't see why," Tom objected. "He may have been counting in the expected one"—but Pascoe dismissed this objection as too frivolous for notice.

"I pretended to believe him, and told him I was very sorry and hoped he would soon find work. Then he thanked me and said he wished there were more people like me in the world. He said he was sure my father must be very proud of me, and my mother too, for they had every reason to be: and in the end he asked me for the price of a pint."

"Goodness!" Tom exclaimed. Again he wanted to laugh, but instinct warned him that if he did he would hear no more.

"I asked him how much the price of a pint was," Pascoe continued gravely, "and he told me sixpence. But I expect my asking him may have raised his hopes, for when I said I hadn't got sixpence, nor indeed any money at all, he suddenly turned nasty, and wanted to know what I meant by wasting his time. In fact he called me two very bad words, which I think I'd better not repeat, though I dare say you've heard them before."

"I didn't ask you to repeat them," Tom replied; and since Pascoe appeared to have concluded his story he took him to the spot he had thought of for the aquarium, and from there up to the loft to see the aquarium itself.

The loft was a long, low, whitewashed room, lit by a skylight and by a broad window facing the cobbled yard. They climbed up to it from the interior of the motor-house by means of a board with footholes in it, at the top of which was an open trap-door. Its only furniture was a plain solid kitchen table and a couple of chairs, but Pascoe's attention was immediately caught by the railway spread out on the floor, and it was with some difficulty that Tom drew him from this to more important business. "There it is," he said, pointing to the bath, "and what we've got to do is to get it down. I've tied ropes round it, because we'll have to lower it out of the window; the trap-door's too small."

Even with the window pushed up as high as it would go, it looked as if it might be a narrow squeeze, though, as Pascoe observed, if it had been possible to get the bath into the loft, it must be equally possible to get it out again; and he examined the ropes himself, testing each knot carefully in spite of Tom's repeated assurances. Fortunately the window-ledge was level with the floor, so there would be no hoisting to be done, for the bath was an old-fashioned iron one and remarkably heavy. They pushed it nearly half-way through the window, where it remained poised. "We'd better stand well back," said the prudent Pascoe. "And jolly well mind what you're doing, because it'll give the most frightful jerk once it gets over."

"We can't both stand back, or how are we to push it?" Tom objected, and they were still discussing the problem when Phemie came out into the yard and saw them.

"What are you at now, Master Tom?" she cried in alarm. "Don't you push that bath another inch, or you'll be down after it. . . . Do you hear what I'm telling you . . . ? Wait—I'm coming."

They waited, and Phemie hurriedly crossed the yard and disappeared inside the motor-house. Next moment they heard her laboriously climbing the footboard, for the holes were far apart, and Phemie was stout and hampered by her skirts. Presently her head and shoulders emerged through the trap-door, and they both rushed to her assistance. "Get out of me way," she snapped at them, "I can manage better by myself."

Manage she did, though with much puffing and blowing; and the moment she recovered sufficient breath she began to scold them both impartially, regardless of the fact that she had never seen Pascoe before. Tom tried to explain why they wanted to get the bath down, but she continued to speak her mind, while Pascoe gazed at her with solemn blue eyes. He seemed surprised at Phemie's extremely frank remarks, but Tom wasn't, and moreover knew they wouldn't prevent her from helping them, and that with this powerful aid the job of lowering the bath would be child's play. It was at any rate successful, for there was not even a bump when it reached the ground. "Thanks awfully, Phemie dear," Tom said affectionately, while Pascoe expressed a more reserved gratitude.

The task concluded, Phemie recovered her good humour. "We'll help you down," Tom assured her, but the proffered aid again was refused, though this time more graciously. "Run on now, the both of you—and don't be waiting in the garridge eether, for I know I'll be a sight, with them steps near a yard apart." So they left her, and hovered discreetly just outside the door till she had accomplished the descent. "She's frightfully decent, isn't she?" Tom whispered to Pascoe. "Of course we could have got it down by ourselves in the long run, but it was decent of her all the same, and it saved a lot of bother."

Possibly Phemie overheard these commendations, or guessed them; at all events she continued her good offices by helping them to convey the bath—balanced on the largest wheelbarrow—to its destination. There she left them, amid a shower of renewed thanks. "She's as strong as a horse," Tom murmured in admiration, as he gazed after her broad back. "She's got arms like the Japanese wrestlers in Granny's picture. She broke the kitchen range one day when she was cleaning it, and *it's* solid iron."

This feat—much, if less appreciatively, commented on at the time by Mother—had greatly impressed him, but Pascoe received it absent-mindedly, for he was thinking of the aquarium. The dogs had already examined this in their own fashion.

"We'll get a spade—two spades—and the thing William uses for cutting edges—it's as sharp as a knife."

They ran to the tool-house, accompanied by Roger and Pincher, while lazy old Barker stretched himself alongside the upturned bath, knowing very well they would soon come back.

"We'd better use the wheelbarrow," Pascoe deliberated, "and put the sods and earth in that. It'll save time and won't make a mess of the grass all round."

Tom agreed; and Pascoe, with the edge-cutter, began at once to outline the cavity they had to dig. He did this with the greatest skill and neatness, as if he had been accustomed to such jobs all his life. Indeed, the superiority of his workmanship was so patent that Tom soon left all the nicer part to him, and even William, whom curiosity presently brought along to see what mischief they were up to, emitted a grunt of approval.

Pascoe alone was not satisfied. "What we need is a beetle, to pound the bottom firm and hard; and a spirit-level too, if we're to get it really right."

"I'll get the——" Tom was beginning, when to his amazement William interrupted him with, "Bide you where you are;" and stalked off.

"He's gone to get them!" Tom marvelled. "At least I believe he has. I bet he wouldn't have got them for me."

He was still pondering on this strange phenomenon when William returned with both beetle and spirit-level. These he handed to Pascoe: to Tom he merely gave instructions to put them back in the tool-house "when the young gentleman has finished with them." After which, he left them to their labours, the most difficult of these being to graduate the slope of the sides to fit the shape of the bath.

It took time, but they both worked hard, and had practically completed the task when Mother came out to invite Pascoe to stay to lunch. "Well, I must say," she exclaimed, "you've done it very neatly! I wonder how much of the neatness is due to—— You haven't told me your friend's name yet, Tom."

"Pascoe," said Tom, who had told her dozens of times.

"I don't mean that. You can hardly expect me to call him Pascoe."

This left Tom at a loss, for he had never thought of any other name. It turned out, too, to be an extremely footling one—Clement—though that of course wasn't Pascoe's fault.

Before she went, just to give Mother an idea of how spacious the aquarium was, Tom decided to put all three dogs in it together. "Look, Mother!"—and he called them.

Mother looked; so did Pascoe; both standing back in order to give Tom and his dogs a free field. The obliging animals immediately approached, wagging their tails. Standing in a row and regarding him with affection, they listened attentively to what he told them; but for all that, they paused on the brink. Tom was surprised. "Don't be so silly," he said; and to prove the aquarium was all right, got into it himself. The dogs watched him benevolently—Barker sitting down to do so—and Pascoe and Mother began to laugh.

If they hadn't laughed Tom might have abandoned his attempt, but now he was determined. So, apparently, were the dogs, though they evinced the greatest good nature, and Barker, who was perhaps growing bored or absent-minded, offered a paw. Tom tried first persuasion and then physical force, but neither availed. He might lift them in, but while they permitted this with a touching docility, they jumped out again so quickly that still there was never more than one in at a time, and Pascoe, when called upon to help, proved useless. Very nervously he lifted Pincher, choosing him because he was the smallest; but at the first growl he hastily set him down again.

"I think you'd better leave them, dear, and come in and get ready for lunch," Mother said. "They evidently don't like it."

"Wait just a minute," Tom begged, but Mother had waited quite long enough, and since she now left them and returned to the house, there was no point in continuing the demonstration.

"I wonder *why* they won't get in?" Tom murmured, puzzled. Pascoe suggested that it was because they were stupid, but to this Tom shook his head. "Well—the next thing, I suppose, is to get water; and we'll have to carry it in cans, for the hose wouldn't reach half-way."

Pascoe, who with his hands in his pockets was contemplating their morning's work, did not at once reply, and when he did, it was to say that that wasn't the next thing. "If you fill it with water now, you'll only have to empty it again."

"Why?" Tom asked, for he was impatient to see what it would look like. There could be no denying that it still closely resembled a bath; but by planting moss— Or perhaps stones, with rock plants, would be better. . . .

"I went down town on Saturday afternoon," Pascoe continued—"to the library; and looked up aquariums in the Encyclopedia; and you ought to make a gravel bed at the bottom, and plant water weeds in it to keep the water pure. Real aquariums have running water, but it says the other will do; and snails help too. If the water isn't kept fresh it gets an awful smell and all the things die. But it doesn't do to change it; that's just as bad; so we'll plant weeds and get a lot of snails."

Tom felt a little annoyed that he hadn't thought of looking up the Encyclopedia himself. He also felt, or was beginning to suspect, that his part in the aquarium was going to be a secondary one—that of assistant to the more efficient and thorough Pascoe. Not that he really minded. Pascoe wasn't like Max Sabine; there was nothing bossy or superior about him. "We'll get gravel from the stream in the glen after lunch," he said; "and we'd better go in now, for I have to look after the dogs' dinner."

Later, when they were seated at the table, it became clear to him that Mother had taken a liking to Pascoe. Somehow this faintly amused him, he didn't know why. He himself thought Pascoe was jolly decent, but at the same time there were certain things about him that made it quite easy to understand Brown's attitude. Boys like Brown were bound to think him a bit of a squirt, and once or twice during the morning Tom had not been wholly exempt from this feeling himself. For one thing, Pascoe sometimes talked—was talking now for instance—in the most frightfully grown-up way; never raising his voice or getting excited; never interrupting, though Mother sometimes took a long time to say what she wanted to say, because this usually reminded her of a lot of other things which she had to deal with before getting back to the main thing, so that now and then she had to ask you what that was.

Daddy never interrupted her either, but it wasn't the same. He simply sat there with a look of resignation on his face, as different as possible from Pascoe's polite attention. Anyhow, Mother was growing more and more pleased with him. She hoped he would be able to spend the rest of the day with Tom, because she and Daddy were going out after tea and wouldn't be back till fairly late in the evening. There wouldn't be any regular dinner for them, but Phemie would see to it that at least they weren't starved.

"High tea," Tom thought; and it would be good fun having it by themselves. He would pour out. Mary of course would want to, but he wouldn't let her. It was disappointing, therefore, when Pascoe said he must go home soon after lunch, because he was being taken into town to get a new suit of clothes. He promised, on the other hand, to stay as long as he could, and this so positively that it caused Mother to reverse her invitation. She now thought he ought to be home by three o'clock at the latest, since Mrs. Pascoe might have a number of things to do in town, and he certainly oughtn't to keep her waiting.

"That means we'd better put off getting the gravel till to-morrow," Tom said. "But I can show you the stream now; there's tons of time for that."

Out in the garden, he collected the dogs and took Pascoe through the side door leading to the glen, where they all scrambled down to the water's edge. Here they followed the stream, through chequered sunlight and leafy shadows, noting where in its broken course there were beds of fine sand and gravel. "We'll have to bring buckets, and it'll take a good many journeys, for we won't be able to carry more than half a bucketful at a time, gravel's so heavy. . . ." Suddenly he broke off. "Oh, don't let Pincher drink or he'll be sick! Pincher! Pincher! Good dog . . . ! Now stay there or you'll get a smack. . . . He always *will* drink after his dinner, and it gives him indigestion, and then he's sick. It doesn't matter so much at home, because later on he eats it up again, but here it would all be wasted."

Pascoe looked disgusted, and Tom thought he must be terribly sensitive, for he himself could see nothing disgusting about it. To rectify matters, he hastened to explain what actually happened. "It's quite clean: it comes out exactly the way it was when he swallowed it—perfectly smoothly—just the way meat comes out of a mincing-machine. And it's only his dinner: you wouldn't notice the slightest difference really, except that it's perhaps a bit more mixed up and in the shape of a sausage."

"Oh for goodness' sake!" Pascoe exclaimed. "You'd make anybody ill the way you talk!"

"I wouldn't," Tom answered indignantly. "If you're so easily made ill you won't be much good as a scientist."

"It's nothing to do with science," Pascoe returned disdainfully. "I'm not going to be a vet."

Meanwhile Roger and Barker had been splashing up and down the stream—particularly Barker. Except in an occasional pool the water wasn't deep enough for swimming, but they both liked wading, and nosing about after fugitive scents. "We'll not bring them when we're collecting," Pascoe muttered, "or we won't get a thing." He sat down on a fallen tree-trunk and Tom sat beside him. "I don't know that this stream will be much good anyhow," Pascoe went on—"not nearly so good as a pond, or even the river. We want tadpoles for one thing, and there are none here."

"There are spricks though," Tom said, "and I know a pond where there are plenty of tadpoles. There are little eels, too, in the river—whole shoals of them—and they're quite easy to catch if you don't frighten them."

"We'll get some, but we chiefly want tadpoles, so that we can watch them changing into frogs. In a book called *Pond Life* it says there's a kind that turns into newts, but I don't expect you get them in this country. They're quite common in England, but you never get anything in this country: it's the worst possible country for naturalists. . . . Look!"

The last word came in so vehement a whisper that it would have been a hiss had it contained a sibilant. At the same time he had grabbed Tom by the arm and was staring up at the opposite bank of the glen. Tom, momentarily startled, also turned in that direction, and saw between the trees—about twenty yards away and at the very top of the bank—the figure of a man watching them. "It's him," Pascoe whispered. "*Now*, what do you say?"

Actually Tom said nothing, it was Pincher who gave tongue. He remained where he was, however, pressed against Tom's legs, and the other dogs didn't even bark. Nevertheless, the man, who could only have been there for a minute or two, retreated out of sight.

So absorbed had both boys been in planning, making, and discussing their aquarium, that it had driven every other thought out of their heads and they had forgotten all about the burglar. But now even Tom could not help thinking there might be something in Pascoe's idea. They sat in silence till the latter, still speaking in a whisper, asked: "Why has he been lurking about all this time? What has he been doing—or do you think he's been away and come back again?"

Tom couldn't imagine; it certainly looked queer; though he

still had not quite adopted Pascoe's sinister view. "He may have been over at Denny's—doing some job—and they may have given him his dinner: they're very decent—especially Mrs. Denny."

"It's taken him a long time to eat it then," Pascoe replied. "But perhaps now he's seen the dogs he'll clear off permanently. . . . I wonder if he knows your father and mother are going out for the evening."

"How could he know?" Tom exclaimed. "I didn't even know myself. And if he was really spying, as you say, he must have seen the dogs before. Anyhow Phemie and Mary will be there; and I thought your idea was that he was going to break into the house in the middle of the night."

Nevertheless, Pascoe's last remark suggested to him a scheme, which he determined to put into practice. If nothing else, at least it would be good fun; and he might never have the opportunity, or at any rate so good an excuse, again.

"If I were you," Pascoe was saying, "I'd tell your mother before she goes out. I'd come with you myself, only I ought to be going home. It must be precious near three o'clock already, if not after it."

He got up as he spoke, and Tom and the dogs accompanied him to see him off. "I'll come over to-morrow," Pascoe promised, and finally, before mounting his bicycle, he repeated still more urgently his advice about telling Mother.

CHAPTER XIV

Tom waited until Pascoe was out of sight before turning away. But he did not go back to the house, he followed the road for some fifty yards till he reached a five-barred gate. This he climbed, and was in the fields.

The cool breeze which had freshened the morning had now died down, and the hot sun brought out powerfully the heavy drowsy scents of whin and meadow-sweet. It was a lazy, sleepy afternoon, Tom thought. And in harmony with it, he himself felt agreeably lazy, as he loitered along the deeply-rutted cart-track skirting the outlying fields of Denny's farm. These stretched away on his right, while on his left was a broad ditch with a high bank topped by a tangled hedge of hawthorn, honeysuckle, and briar, broken at intervals by trees—ash, willow, or oak—and by rough grey boulders stained with moss and lichen. The dogs plunged in and out of the ditch, which was at present dry, innumerable plants having drawn up its moisture—vetches, cow-parsley, ragged-robbin and foxgloves. The ferns and ivy, which would gradually darken as summer advanced, were still vividly green; and the leaves of the trees had a similar freshness—narrow oval willow leaves, serrated oak leaves, shining beech leaves, and cool delicate ash sprays. A cawing of rooks floated from the direction of the farm-house half a mile away.

The dogs were hunting, but in a desultory fashion, and they raised nothing. Suddenly Pincher disappeared down a cavernous rabbit-hole. Tom had known he would, for every time they passed that way the same thing happened. The hole had been abandoned long ago, and Pincher must have known this, but it possessed an irresistible fascination for him, and by frequent excavations he had so widened the entrance that now it would nearly have admitted Tom himself. The pertinacious Pincher had even managed to turn a corner, so that only his tail and frantically-working hind-legs were visible amid the showers of sand he scattered behind him. Tom, standing above the hole, could hear his fore-paws scratching underground, and wondered how he prevented the sand from getting into his eyes. He must keep them shut, he supposed, for it never did; and then, through the noise Pincher was making, he heard very faint little squeals. *Something* alive was there—something much smaller than a rabbit—and he tried to get Pincher to come out.

But this was difficult, and before he had succeeded in gripping him, Pincher emerged backwards of his own accord, holding in his mouth a wretched little mouse, whom Tom hastened to rescue. He was too late; the mouse appeared to be dead; and yet

Tom, examining the tiny body closely while he stroked it with one finger, could discover no wound. The mouse *might* not be dead, for he remembered once rescuing a young thrush from a cat, and the thrush had lain unconscious just like this, yet after a few minutes had suddenly recovered and flown away. Perhaps the mouse too would recover, though mice were much more easily killed than birds, and Pincher was rough and clumsy, not in the least like a cat.

He lifted the body and laid it on the grass under some dock leaves where he could keep an eye on it and see that Pincher, who had been very good about giving it up, did not return to have another look. The dogs at first waited with him, but presently, knowing he would not go home without them, wandered on. They still kept to the bank, because it was pitted with innumerable rabbit-holes, and though the inhabitants of these at the first alarm had all scuttled into safety, everywhere enticing smells were calling for investigation.

Tom, left alone, retreated a few yards into the deep green meadow, which looked cool and inviting, though actually he would have found it cooler in the ditch itself. Lying on his back, he gazed up through the tall feathery grass at the sky, and nibbled a leaf of crimson-seeded sorrel. Now that Daddy and Mother were gone out for the evening, he thought it would be pleasant to stay here till the moon rose, and wished he had brought some provisions with him, and also his mouth-organ. He plucked a clover-blossom and tried to suck out the honey, but the quantity he could extract was so small that it left no more than a faint ghost of sweetness on his tongue. . . .

It was very still—so still that when he listened attentively he could hear stealthy movements in the unmown grass all round him, where a hidden life was in full activity. Perhaps this activity ceased at night, but just now there was an extraordinary busyness, as if all these minute creatures were intent each on his own private work—getting food, looking after eggs, bringing up families—and hadn't a minute to waste in idleness. A very big beetle—broad, polished, and black as ebony—climbed on to the back of Tom's open hand, clutching it with sharp little feet, as if with the friendliest intention. A bumble-bee alighted on the tuft of clover from which he had plucked his flower, and like the beetle, he looked enormous—which was strange, seeing that the mouse, who was really much bigger than either of them, had looked extremely small. Perhaps, when you came to consider them, most things were strange, Tom thought. It was strange, doubtless, that he should feel sure that the bumble-bee was a very simple and good-natured person, and the beetle affectionate—for this latter feeling was produced entirely by the grip of his tiny feet. No, not entirely; because there was no reason why the beetle should have climbed on to Tom's hand unless he had wanted to be friends. . . .

He began to grow drowsy, and the endless summer murmur whispered in his ear, "Sleepy-head, sleepy-head, go to sleep." An orange-tipped butterfly, wavering past, hovered for a moment above him, as if uncertain whether or not to alight: from the far side of the meadow came the peculiar wooden "crake—crake" of the corncrakes calling to one another; and once, from still farther off, he heard the harsh cry of a heron. By and by he heard the movements of what must be some quite large animal in the grass, and cautiously raised himself to look. A hare had come out on to the cart-track not more than three yards away, so that when he raised his head, Tom could clearly see his nostrils working. He tried hard, by wishing, to make the hare come to him, but instead he suddenly bounded across the ditch and was gone. . . .

Tom had forgotten all about the mouse, and must have been lying there dreaming for quite a long time before he next remembered him and went to look. The mouse, too, was gone. . . .

Well, that was a good thing at any rate. The mouse now would be able to tell his wife and children of the terrible adventure he had had. Tom could imagine him repeating the story again and again until the mother mouse said, "You've told us that before, dear," when he would relapse into offended silence. . . .

The bumble-bees must have their nest under the twisted roots of that old thorn-tree, where they were flying in and out. It was a good place, the entrance being hidden by a bramblebush. Close by, under a flat mossy stone, there must certainly be a colony of ants, for he could see several on the stone itself. He partially raised it, and there they were—plunged instantaneously into commotion, scuttling off in every direction with their precious eggs, which must be saved at all costs. It was extraordinary how every creature, down to the very smallest, immediately knew what to do in an emergency. Their efforts might not always be successful, but they never failed to grasp the one chance of success.

Was it cleverness? Frogs, Pascoe declared, always came back to spawn in the pond where they had been born as tadpoles. When they grew up into frogs they scattered over the countryside, but they always came back to spawn in their own pond, though it might be half a mile or a mile or even two miles off. How did they find their way . . . ? And the three swallows' nests under the eaves of the stables at home—every year the same swallows came back to them. Distance did not seem to matter. They did not have to search about, but came directly, unerringly, like a needle to a magnet. It couldn't be cleverness; cleverness wouldn't help in the least. Miss Sabine said it was instinct, and instinct, she said, was inherited memory; but she had been unable to tell him why swallows had inherited a memory so good that it could guide them all the way from Egypt to the exact spot in Ballysheen where their nests were. He didn't believe it was memory at all. Mother's view, that they had simply been created by God with a special gift, seemed far more satisfactory, though it didn't explain how the gift worked. . . .

Here was old Roger back again. That was like him. Tom had known he would be the first to come back, just to make sure that all was well. Roger was a good dog, "lovely and pleasant in his ways", like Saul and Jonathan in the Bible: though Saul hadn't been so lovely and pleasant when he had thrown javelins at David. Pincher would be the next to come: both Roger and Pincher would search for him a long time rather than go home without him.

Barker wouldn't. At least he might or he mightn't—it all depended on whether he got bored or not. If he got bored he would be just as likely to trot quietly home by himself. Tom could never tell how much Barker liked him, and there was no use asking him, for he wouldn't say. . . .

He whistled, and at the third or fourth whistle Pincher came bursting through the hedge, evidently having been hunting on the farther side. But still no Barker. It was getting late too, so Tom turned slowly homeward, though he didn't care for this way of doing things, and paused every few yards to repeat his whistle. But he might have saved his breath, for, as he had half expected, the very first object to meet his eyes when he turned in at the gate was Barker himself, reclining peacefully beside a croquet-hoop. Why did he behave like that? Tom couldn't understand it. Yet neither could he accuse Barker of having abandoned the party, for he hadn't, he was waiting for them here, and the very way he rose now, with a friendly wag of his stumpy tail, showed an untroubled conscience. Tom sighed, and thought how different Roger was—and even Pincher. He brought the whole lot of them into the house to keep him company while he was at tea, and though Mary shook her head, he knew this was merely perfunctory and meant nothing. What was much less perfunctory was her exclamation, "Well of all——!" followed by an eloquent silence, when she came in later to clear the table. Yet there was really nothing to exclaim at, except that, so far as food was concerned, a clearance had already been effected. Mary shoo'd the replete and torpid Pincher out of her way, remarking while she did so that Master Sabine had called early in the afternoon.

Tom's face darkened. He pushed away his plate and pushed back his chair. "What did he want?" he asked petulantly. He had known, of course, that Max would be coming home very soon, but he had forgotten; and in sudden anxiety he added; "You didn't tell him about the aquarium, did you?"

Mary replied that she had told him nothing. "It was the mistress he was talking to; and he only stayed a wee minute anyhow, so perhaps it was just a message he brought."

Tom was only partially reassured. The aquarium belonged exclusively to himself and Pascoe, and he wasn't going to have

Max butting in so long as he could keep him out. He could make an aquarium of his own if he wanted one, and he determined to tell Pascoe to-morrow that under no circumstances was Max to be encouraged.

Calling the dogs, he went out to make sure that everything was as he had left it, and also to pass the time till he could put his plan for the night into action. It was really quite a simple plan—or at least it would be if only Mary and Phemie would take it into their heads to go for a walk. But with Mother and Daddy both out he supposed there wasn't much chance of this, and he daren't overtly suggest it for fear of arousing suspicion. He *had* mentioned to Mary what a beautiful evening it was, yet even that had drawn from her a suspicious glance. It was pretty rotten when you couldn't make a remark about the weather without being credited with ulterior motives. . . .

Anyhow, the initial step, which had consisted in giving the dogs a good solid meal that would last them till morning, was safely accomplished: the second—which was to smuggle them secretly up to his bedroom—would be much more ticklish, for here the slightest hitch would prove fatal. Roger and Barker he thought he could count on, but he was not so sure of Pincher. It might be better to explain the exact scheme to them beforehand, since after all you never knew—or at least Tom never knew—how much of what you said they understood.

So he sat down on a bench under the study window, and got all three dogs before him in a row. Then, very slowly and distinctly, he told them his plan. They listened—Pincher, as usual, cocking his head on one side to do so—and at the conclusion all wagged their tails in approval. So far so good; the plan appeared to have been passed unanimously: on the other hand it had yet to be put into action.

Twilight was drawing on. The new moon, like a slender silver bow, had risen in a fading sky, and pallid moths were flickering in ghostly flight above the rose-bushes. Two or three bats wheeled round the trees, uttering faint yet shrill squeakings as they seized their prey. Not every ear could catch that high note, but Mother's could, and so could Tom's. Presently, breaking in on the quietness, came the noise of the gate opening and closing, and a few seconds later he saw the Sabines' maid approaching up the drive. This was better luck than he could have hoped for, and most cordially he returned her "Good evening" as she passed on round to the back of the house. She must have come, he guessed, to see Phemie and Mary, and being well acquainted with the conversational powers of all three, he knew he could now take a whole regiment of dogs upstairs without attracting attention.

It might, nevertheless, be just as well to seize the opportunity at once, while the going was good; so he gathered his flock around him and cautiously approached and opened the hall door. The flock followed with equal caution—in fact not only behaved, but looked, so extremely like conspirators, that it was quite clear they must have understood his lecture. Noiselessly all four ascended the stairs, but it was not till they were safely in his own room that Tom at last breathed a sigh of satisfaction. So did Pincher, who immediately jumped on to the bed, though the others, better-mannered, remained standing on the floor. Then Tom remembered that he hadn't drunk his glass of milk, which he must do, or Phemie and Mary might think he was still out and go in search of him. Telling the dogs therefore to be good, he ran downstairs, hastily swallowed the milk, and left a pencilled scrawl beside the glass to say he had gone to bed. . . .

When he returned to his room Roger and Barker, influenced no doubt by Pincher's bad example, were now also on the bed, while Pincher himself had found an even more luxurious resting-place on the pillow. It was extraordinary how quickly they had grasped the situation and made their preparations for the night. All the same, these preparations would have to be modified. "I suppose I'm to sleep in a chair," Tom said sarcastically, "or on the floor"—but the only effect of his irony was a partial unclosing of eyes, and a faint movement of tails in drowsy acquiescence; nobody budged.

Tom undressed, put on his pyjamas, and knelt down to say his prayers. These consisted of two short prose prayers and a hymn; but Barker, who was nearest, kept snuffing at his hair in a most distracting way, so he hastily finished and rose from his knees.

"How do you expect me to get in?" he asked, as he stood beside them. "Here, Pincher, you come off that pillow at any rate!—and you'd better all get down for a minute."

They did so, Roger and Pincher at once, Barker more reluctantly and with an audible grumble. But Tom wasn't going to have any nonsense of that sort and gave him a shove. Then he slid between the sheets, settled himself, patted the counterpane, and next moment was nearly smothered under an avalanche of dogs.

By degrees, however, after some pushing and pawing, all found suitable places, and for a while peace reigned. Yet, though the dogs appeared to have fallen asleep almost instantly, Tom, for some reason, had never felt wider awake, and moreover it seemed a pity, in fact a positive waste of this golden opportunity, to go to sleep so soon. Down below, he heard Phemie and Mary coming out of the kitchen with their visitor, and from the fact that shortly afterwards he heard them closing the hall door and coming out into the garden, he guessed that they must have seen his note, and now intended to walk back with her to the Rectory. He listened to the sound of their receding voices and footsteps, and a few seconds later to the distant clang of the gate. They were gone—probably for an hour at least—a fine chance for Pascoe's burglar if he had known—and if he actually existed. . . .

But as yet it was much too early for burglars, whether real or imaginary: certainly things couldn't have worked out better. The dogs, to be sure, appeared to have settled down for the night, but that could soon be altered. In the grey cold light of the quarter-moon their slumbering forms were dimly visible—Roger and Barker on either side of him, Pincher down near his feet. Therefore the first thing to do was to make rats of his feet—rats moving stealthily beneath the bedclothes.

"Rats!" Tom said aloud, and Pincher trembled, cocking one ear out of dreamland, but otherwise not stirring.

"Rats!" Tom said again, and at the repetition the rats themselves made so vigorous an upheaval that Pincher could no longer ignore them. He raised his head, but at the same time he yawned. Very well he knew that these were no true rats, but only Tom's feet. Still, since it seemed to be expected of him and a game was always a game, he made a pounce. After that there was no more sleep for anybody, even the sedate Barker joining in the hunt.

The rat hunt was merely a prelude—designed to remove constraint and set things going; the next item was choral singing. Tom himself had taught them this, only hitherto it had been practised out of doors; within four walls it was infinitely more telling. The volume of sound was indeed remarkable. What it was all about—that is to say, the precise subject of the song—he had never been able to discover; though that it was in essence religious, a sort of hymn to some great invisible spirit—Universal Pan very likely—seemed indicated by its fervour. Yet to-night Tom was inclined to a more secular interpretation. True, he still couldn't make out the exact words, the din was too great, but with a little assistance from his imagination he could fancy them going something like this, the influence of Pincher being unmistakable, especially in the last lines:

Who's got a bone for Barker?
Who's got a bone for he?
A comic old dog and a larker,
Most excellent companee:
So who's got a bone for Barker,
A juicy Be Oh En Eee?

Who's got a bone for Pincher?
A bone with a bit of meat.
Bad luck to the one that would stint yer
Of things for to drink and to eat:
So who's got a bone for Pincher?
Who wants for to give him a treat?

Who's got a bone for Roger?
Roger's the pick of the lot;
An honest old dog, not a dodger;
So fish out a bone from the pot.
Is it deaf that you are, y'ould cod yer—
Bones is bones, whether cold or hot.

* * * * *

"Tom!"

The door had opened, the light was on, and Mother stood there, her face and whole attitude expressive of mingled consternation, astonishment, and displeasure. A profound silence ensued. The dogs hung their heads and looked guilty; Tom looked *very* guilty; and Mother—a most unexpected apparition, for she ought to have been miles away—paused, as if to allow this accumulated sense of guilt to sink well in. . . .

They must have come home early! Had Daddy heard the noise? He could hardly help hearing it, though evidently he had driven the car on round to the garage, leaving Mother to deal with the situation.

She proceeded to do so, while the culprits gazed at her, mute and conscience-stricken. "You're an extremely naughty boy! We came back early because Daddy has a bad headache, and this is what we find! Phemie and Mary both out; and you with the dogs on your bed, though you know very well you're not allowed to bring them upstairs. Just look at that counterpane! Not only filthy dirty, but with a great rent in it!"

Tom looked, and could not deny that the counterpane had suffered, though till Mother had turned on the light he had not been aware of it. The rats, he supposed—Pincher was always so careless! But he had never been told not to bring the dogs up to bed with him; possibly because nobody had ever dreamed that he would do so. Still, the fact remained, and he hastened to point it out to Mother. Instantly she asked him; "Did you think I would allow you to bring them up?"—a question admitting of only one answer.

On the other hand, he had had a special reason to-night, which made all the difference, and he proceeded to relate the story of the burglar.

She listened, yet though he tried his hardest to impart to it something of Pascoe's impressiveness, it did not appear to be impressing Mother. Instead of comment, when he had finished she simply asked a further question, which, if answered truthfully, would nullify everything he had said. "Did you really think a burglar was going to break into the house?"

"I—I—I thought—perhaps Pascoe thought so."

It sounded feeble—very, very feeble—and he knew it. So, from their dejected attitudes, he gathered, did the dogs. "In that case, why did you let Phemie and Mary go out?" Mother said. "And why didn't you tell me about it before *I* went out?"

"Pascoe advised me to tell you," Tom put in eagerly.

"Yet you didn't. Why?"

"I—I thought——"

Mother waited rather grimly, and then answered for him. "Yes; you thought that if you didn't it would be a good excuse for keeping the dogs with you."

Since this was the exact truth, Tom could only try to look injured.

"Well, they're going home now at all events," Mother continued firmly. "And I'm very much disappointed: I thought I could have trusted you."

"But it's so late," Tom pleaded.

"It's not a bit late," Mother replied; and after a further look at the counterpane added ominously: "I don't know what Daddy will say to all this!"

Tom didn't either, and remained silent until he murmured with deep feeling, "Poor Daddy! Don't you think it might make his headache worse to be worried—I mean, if you told him?"

This sudden sympathy, instead of mending matters, appeared to have precisely the opposite effect. "Don't be a little hypocrite," Mother answered sharply. "Much you care about Daddy's headache! And at any rate he knows already: we heard the

was still further tickled when she came out, talked to the burglar, and eventually called William to see if he could find something for him to do. William then took him in tow, and both went round to the yard.

Pascoe had watched all this coldly from a distance, but disappointingly made no comment when Tom rejoined him. Instead, he remarked, "We're wasting time," with the air of one whose patience, though great, is not inexhaustible. "He's as obstinate as a mule," Tom thought, yet not without a certain appreciation, as they collected the buckets and went down to the stream.

While they worked, toiling to and fro between the stream and the aquarium, his cogitations shifted from the burglar to Max Sabine. It was three months now since he had last seen Max, but he gladly would have extended the period indefinitely. True, there was no particular reason why he should expect him to-day, except that he had called yesterday—on the pretext, Mother said, of looking for Pincher. Nevertheless Tom felt sure he *would* come. . . . That is to say, supposing he could find nothing better to do—his visits had always been contingent upon this. Certainly the fact that they had quarrelled violently on their last meeting would not deter him. . . .

The quarrel had not been altogether for the reason Althea supposed. That, indeed, had been the climax, but there had been several unpleasant incidents before the James-Arthur episode had finally opened Tom's eyes. Max might think he had forgotten, but he hadn't: he had made up his mind last April to have nothing more to do with him, and his determination remained unchanged. It seemed, therefore, the moment to warn Pascoe. He had already done so more or less, but it could do no harm to be a little more explicit. "Of course he mayn't come," he wound up, after a brief summary of the situation—"but if he does, don't be letting him interfere, which is what he'll want to do."

Pascoe had set down his bucket, glad of a temporary rest, for they were both by this time wet and weary. "What's he like?" he asked.

Tom with difficulty concealed his irritation. He had already told Pascoe what Max was like, and he now added pointedly: "He's like Brown, only far worse." Not that he himself had the least feeling against Brown, but because he knew from past experience that Max's first aim would be to try to establish an understanding with Pascoe, and he thought this would be the best way to guard against such an alliance. Unwarned, Pascoe was far too simple to realize Max's cunning: in fact, if left to himself, he would be a lamb in his hands, because for all his cleverness Pascoe was really as innocent as a baby, and Max could be most ingratiating.

They worked all morning without interruption, and by lunch-time the aquarium was finished, filled with water, and ready to receive its destined inhabitants. Pascoe, having conscientiously repeated a message from home to the effect that Mrs. Barber wasn't to allow him to be a nuisance, again accepted an invitation to lunch, during which meal Mother had a lot to tell them about the new man, who evidently had poured out all his misfortunes to her. His name was Patrick Keady, and according to Mother, or rather according to the story he had told her—for she was going to make further inquiries before accepting it as gospel—he was a most domestic and virtuous character, out of employment through no fault of his own, and, like other unskilled labourers, finding it very difficult to get a fresh start. At this point Tom couldn't resist glancing at Pascoe, expecting to see him looking a little abashed; but not a bit of it; Pascoe, prim and demure as ever, returned the glance with his usual calm and steady gaze. The extraordinary thing was that Mother did not appear to have identified her protégé with their burglar, or else, since this seemed scarcely credible, was deliberately avoiding that aspect of the subject in order to spare Pascoe's feelings. She needn't have worried, Tom could have told her; there was a sort of "Time-will-show" expression on Pascoe's face, which plainly indicated that he still held to his first opinion.

As soon as he got him alone, Tom tried to reason with him, pointing out the wretched nature of the evidence which was all he could produce in support of his prejudice; but he had scarcely begun when he broke off abruptly, for at that moment he caught sight of Max. Instantly his face clouded. "Here he is!" he ejaculated in a rapid undertone, while Max, in a self-possessed and leisurely fashion, got off his bicycle, leaned it against a tree, and strolled towards them across the grass.

They watched him, themselves motionless and silent, but their guarded attitude did not appear to embarrass the visitor. "Well, well, well!" he exclaimed jocularly, approaching the aquarium. "What's all this?"—just as if it wasn't perfectly obvious what it was.

Max had grown a lot in the past three months—or at any rate Tom thought so. In contrast with Pascoe and himself he looked tall and languidly elegant; but then of course he was nearly four years older than they were, and had always been given to plastering his hair and trying to make himself look like an illustration in an American magazine. He was supposed by most people to be very handsome—just because he had finely-moulded features, a clear olive skin, and dark sleepy eyes—but Tom disliked his appearance, and particularly disliked his thin-lipped mouth, which he thought unpleasant and sneering. Pascoe meanwhile stood staring at him, as if seeking a resemblance to the notorious Brown—a resemblance certainly not there, Brown being anything but languid, and his dimpled, smiling countenance reflecting at all times an inveterate good-nature.

"It's our aquarium," Tom muttered unwillingly, wishing they had started out at once to collect their specimens, instead of lingering over lunch, discussing Keady and other things with Mother.

Max's smile was the patronizing one of a fully-fledged adolescent schoolboy among kids. He kicked the brim of the bath and remarked: "What's the good of an aquarium with nothing in it? D'you keep it for washing the dogs? Here, Pincher!"—and he threw in the skin of the banana he was eating.

It was no doubt a very mild offence, and coming from anybody else Tom would not have resented it, but now he flushed angrily and grabbed Pincher by the collar before he could move, while Pascoe cried: "Don't!"—and proceeded to fish out the banana skin with his net.

Max turned at the word, as if discovering for the first time that Tom was not alone. "Hello!" he said, raising his eyebrows. "Where did *you* spring from?"

Pascoe blushed, but Tom replied for him. "He didn't spring from anywhere: it's you who sprang. And if you didn't see him till now your eyesight must be defective."

It was an unpromising beginning, and Max, though not in the least disconcerted, evidently decided to alter his tone. "Sorry," he apologized: "I was only ragging."

Tom said nothing, but Pascoe quite unnecessarily began to explain that they had only finished the aquarium that morning, and hadn't had time to stock it yet.

To Tom's secret disappointment, Max immediately dropped his air of superiority and became all friendliness and good humour. "Let's get some things now," he proposed. "What about the mill-dam? It used to be a good place."

The artless Pascoe at once responded to this change of manner. "We didn't think of the mill-dam, did we?" he said to Tom. "I didn't even know there was one. We might have a look at it first—though the book says a pond's the best. Still, a mill-dam might have fish in it"—and to Tom's annoyance he clearly accepted the idea that Max was going to help them: in fact Pascoe was behaving in exactly the way he had been cautioned not to.

"There's a pond there too," Max continued. "At least, it's not far off: I'll show you."

"I can show him," Tom interrupted pugnaciously. "I told him about it yesterday"—for this was his tadpole pond, which he had been reserving as a special surprise. "I suppose you're going for a ride," he went on, though he supposed nothing of the sort.

Nor, apparently, did Max, who merely answered; "No; I think I'll come with you."

Tom was silenced. He knew Max understood him perfectly, but he also knew that (with Pascoe so conspicuously failing to back him up) this would make no difference. Nevertheless he persevered. "We've only got two nets," he said; and this hint also being ignored, he added disagreeably: "Of course, you can carry the bottles."

It was *meant* to be disagreeable, and drew indeed an expostulatory glance from Pascoe; but Max only gave him a peculiar look—not at all pleasant. "Thanks," he drawled, after a deliberate pause. "I think I'll only superintend. . . . You might fall in, you know."

The last words were obviously spoken in mockery, but Pascoe—who really was behaving most stupidly—took them seriously. "The mill-dam, do you mean? Is it deep?"

"Awfully deep," Max replied, "with slimy, slippery sides. If you can't swim, to fall in would be certain death." Then, as Pascoe swallowed this like a glass of milk: "They fished out a man's body last winter, and the eels had eaten his face off, so that they never would have found out who he was if a detective hadn't discovered a masonic sign very faintly tatooed on his chest."

"On his chest!" Pascoe repeated in an awed tone.

"Well, you wouldn't have had it on his——"

"Oh, come on," Tom broke in irritably. "Can't you see he's only stuffing you up?"

He lifted a net and one of the glass jars as he spoke, and they were about to set off when Pascoe suggested that they should leave the dogs behind. "They'll only go splashing about and frightening everything, the way they did yesterday in the stream."

Max glanced sidelong at Tom. "Good idea," he agreed. "We can either leave them here or send them home: they won't mind, and it doesn't much matter if they do."

"Well then," said Pascoe, preparing to start; but abruptly he paused.

For Tom had made no movement to accompany them, but stood there, sullen and hostile, his face black as a thundercloud. "I think you and Max had better go together," he said stiffly to Pascoe; "I'm going with the dogs." And immediately he called them to him, which was hardly necessary, seeing that the faithful creatures were already there and hadn't the slightest intention of leaving him.

Pascoe looked alarmed. He had spoken on impulse, but now he realized his mistake, though still not understanding why Tom should be taking it like this. After all, it wasn't *his* fault that Max was there, and if it came to that, Tom had been just as much to blame as Max for any unpleasantness there had been. However, it was Tom who was his friend; so he said hastily; "We'll bring the dogs"—to which Max added lightly, "The more the merrier."

On this they set off, though, with the exception of Pincher, the only person who appeared to be particularly merry was Max himself, who did most of the talking, and seemed quite unconscious that all was not well. True, he addressed his remarks entirely to Pascoe, but this, in the circumstances, perhaps was not unnatural.

They went down to the river, and crossed by the lock gate to the opposite bank. But for Tom the whole expedition had lost its charm, and he now wished that Max and Pascoe *would* leave him; even his interest in the aquarium had vanished. When they reached the pond the first thing he did was to offer his net to Max, saying he didn't want to fish, and would take the dogs along the river bank and give them a swim.

Max needed no pressing; he simply said "Thanks", and accepted the net; but Pascoe, gazing at Tom dubiously, seemed uncertain what to do. That was his own fault, Tom thought, and he left them, returning to the river, and following it down past the weir to the saw-mill.

This was an ancient and rather primitive construction of rough grey stones, between which bright-green hart's-tongue ferns and crimson valerian and crane's-bill had taken root. They had not only taken root, but had flourished so vigorously that the mill itself appeared to be either emerging from or returning to Nature. In the shadow of its archway the great water-wheel revolved slowly and ponderously with a rumbling noise that made the walls tremble; and from the roof of the arch, in a perpetual twilight, grey stalactites hung down. The water was black as ink, except where it was splashed by the wheel and rose in white showers against the semi-darkness of the cavern beyond; but all around, everything was cool and fresh and green, and Tom, feeling injured, sulky and resentful, lay down in the shade of an ash-tree to brood over his wrongs. Pincher immediately sprawled across his middle, while Roger sat up beside him, and Barker went for a solitary bathe, swimming slowly round and round the dam, occasionally scrambling out to shake himself (when Tom could distinctly hear his ears rattling), but very soon plunging in again. He did all this most solemnly, and yet clearly he was enjoying himself in his own quiet fashion, not troubling his head about what the others did or thought, content if they cared to share his amusement, and equally content if they didn't. . . .

Gradually Tom's mood altered. The rumble and plash of the huge wheel, monotonous and musical, had a tranquillizing effect upon him—lenitive, almost palpable, soothing as oil or balm. Stretched on his back, with his face upturned to the sky, he could not see the wheel; therefore in his imagination it became a living and benevolent monster, guardian of the river and of this green shade. Why were animals—even fabulous and imaginary ones—so much closer to him than human beings? He no longer felt cross, yet neither did he feel the least inclination to rejoin Max and Pascoe. It was they who eventually rejoined him—or rather one of them, for Max, it seemed, had soon grown tired of collecting tadpoles, and suddenly recollecting something much more important he wanted to do, had gone back to the house to get his bicycle, leaving Pascoe to carry the nets and both jam-jars. Pascoe, with a jar in each hand, and the nets tucked under his arm, looked none too pleased by this desertion; but to Tom it was not at all surprising—was in fact just the kind of thing he would have expected from Max.

Pascoe set his burden carefully down on the grass, glanced at Tom with a shade of anxiety, as if not quite certain of his ground, and after a pause asked; "*Are* there any fish in the dam?"

"I don't know; I didn't look."

Another and more prolonged silence followed, and again it was broken by Pascoe. "What were you in such a bait about? I wouldn't have said not to bring the dogs if I'd thought you'd mind. I only meant while we were fishing."

"I know. It wasn't that really. At least it wouldn't have been if he hadn't been there."

"But you were mad with *me*; and I don't see what I had done."

"You didn't do anything. I warned you beforehand what would happen: it's always the same when there's more than one boy there. He makes them quarrel with each other, and he does it on purpose. I told you he had tried to do it with James-Arthur and me, only he didn't succeed. If you'd been alone, or I'd been alone, he'd have been quite different."

"I don't like him much," Pascoe admitted, glancing at the jam-jars.

"He says he has a rook-rifle," he pursued slowly, after another interval, "and that shooting is better sport than making an aquarium. . . . He says he's shot lots of things—birds and rabbits, and a cat. His father gave him the rifle for a birthday present, and thinks there's no harm in shooting—that all healthy-minded boys like it, and that if they don't they must be morbid or something. . . . He offered to let me have a try."

Tom appeared indifferent. "Are you going to?"

"No."

It sounded decisive, yet the word was hardly out of his mouth before the conscientious Pascoe began to fidget uneasily, evidently fearing more might be attached to it than he had actually meant. "It's not that I wouldn't do it," he said, "or that I think shooting's wrong, but——"

"But what?"

"I thought he thought it would annoy you if I did, and that that was really why he offered to let me."

CHAPTER XVI

Awakening in the early morning, Tom had heard the sound of distant drums, but in a minute or two he had dropped off to sleep again, and it was quiet when he awoke once more and this time definitely. Breakfast, he knew, would be earlier than usual, because of the general holiday. It was strange how everything felt so differently on different days. There was a Saturday afternoon feeling, a Sunday feeling, a Monday morning feeling, and there was certainly a twelfth of July feeling. While he was dressing he again caught the far-off beating of drums. William would be walking, and meals would be informal and picnicky, because Phemie and Mary would be getting most of the day off. In the early afternoon Pascoe was to come over, and he and Tom were going to the field to watch the procession. Daddy and Mother might be going too, and there would be speeches—Max's father, who was a great Orangeman, would be making a speech: the field chosen for this year's meeting was only about a mile from the Rectory.

After breakfast he filled a pocket with cherries and went down to the hollow oak to give Edward the squirrel a twelfth of July treat. The whole countryside was deserted, for, except those whom domestic duties confined to the house, and the very smallest of the children, the entire village, dressed in its Sunday clothes, had gone into town holiday-making, though most of them would return in the afternoon in the wake of the great procession.

Tom crossed the meadow and stood beneath the oak. "Edward!" he called, and from the gnarled upper branches a sharp little face with cocked ears and bright eyes peeped down, just to make sure it was the right person. Then Edward descended, leaping swiftly and lightly from branch to branch till he was on a level with Tom's head, when he paused, waiting to see what had been brought to him.

Tom produced a cherry, and Edward, sitting up alertly, took

it in his hands. But being rather greedy, and having caught a glimpse of the store from which this was only a sample, he nibbled it hastily and threw it down half finished. "Here!" said Tom; "that won't do. If you're going to be so wasteful I'll eat them myself." As an example, he lifted the rejected cherry and finished it slowly, while Edward watched him and presumably felt ashamed. After that, they divided the remainder between them, though Edward got very much the lion's share, Tom only eating one now and again to keep him company. There were a few nuts to wind up with, but these Edward carried off one by one to his secret store-room. Finally he perched on Tom's shoulder and allowed himself to be scratched and stroked, till the sound of a voice hallooing from a distance made him spring back into the tree like lightning.

The voice was Pascoe's, and Tom answered with a shrill whistle. Pascoe, still invisible, could be heard scrambling up the bank of the glen, and next moment Roger, who must have picked him up somewhere, burst into the open. Pascoe was not so quick, but very soon he also emerged, waving a small flag, and with an orange lily in his buttonhole. "What are you doing? I've been hunting for you all over the place."

"I was feeding Edward," Tom replied. "You told me you weren't coming till the afternoon."

"I know, and I didn't intend to; but Mother thought if I was riding over I'd better start while the road was clear. . . . Who's Edward?"

"He's a squirrel, and lives in this tree: but you've frightened him and now he's hiding. He'd soon come down, all the same, if Roger wasn't there."

Pascoe gazed up through the branches. "What were you giving him?"

"Cherries. . . . Nuts too; but he puts those away. He's got a storehouse where he keeps acorns and beech-nuts and things like that for the winter. . . . I made a storehouse myself—to keep biscuits in—under a tree in the glen; but Barker and Pincher found it and ate the biscuits, though they were in a tin box. I suppose the lid must have come loose."

"You blame everything on Barker and Pincher," Pascoe said. "How do you know it wasn't Roger? He's with you far more than they are."

"Yes, but he wouldn't; he's got a frightfully sensitive conscience and that makes him different from the others."

Pascoe turned a somewhat sceptical eye on Roger. "He wouldn't know it was *your* storehouse. . . . How could he? And if he didn't, I don't see where the conscience comes in."

"He *would* know. As a matter of fact they all knew; because they were with me when I made it. And Barker and Pincher went straight back that very afternoon and dug out the things and ate them."

"But you didn't *see* them do it," Pascoe argued, "you're only guessing."

"I didn't actually see them," Tom admitted; "I never said I saw them. But who else would do it?"

"Roger."

Tom gave a shrug of impatience. "Haven't I just told you Roger wouldn't—because of his conscience."

Pascoe pointed out that because Tom told him a thing didn't necessarily make it true. "If you're so sure about it," he went on, "you must have seen him some time when he *had* done something he shouldn't. Therefore his conscience can't always keep him from doing things."

"Oh, there's no use talking to you."

"Not if you can't talk reasonably. To hear you, you'd think Roger was perfect—a kind of angel."

This was a new idea, and struck by it, Tom did not reply. He, too, surveyed the dog with a conscience, who finding himself the centre of so much attention, wagged his tail and planted his forepaws against his friend's shoulders. "An angel could take any form he wanted to," Tom murmured dreamily. "Roger might be an angel without anybody knowing—a guardian angel. . . . So might Ralph."

He awoke to find Pascoe's gaze—remorseless as an arc-lamp—fixed searchingly upon him. "Who's Ralph?" Pascoe demanded.

"Nobody," Tom answered. . . . "Just a name I saw."

But Pascoe was not satisfied. "If he's just a name it's queer you should have mentioned him! I suppose you mean you don't want to tell me. Is he somebody you're not allowed to know?"

This was so very likely to be true that Tom couldn't help laughing, though he stopped at once when Pascoe began to look offended. "I would tell you about him, only I know you wouldn't believe."

Pascoe said no more, but there was a cloud on his brow which showed what he thought. Tom, for that matter, disliked reservations and secrecy himself, only he was quite sure Pascoe *wouldn't* believe. He might be credulous where burglars were concerned, but that was different. Burglars belonged definitely to this world—were very much solid flesh and blood, whereas——. On the other hand, he didn't want to seem distrustful and uncommunicative, so he compromised by telling the beginning of the story, without mentioning his adventure at Granny's and its sequel. "Ralph is Ralph Seaford. . . . He died when he was a boy, and there's a stained-glass window put up in memory of him in the church. That's how I know his name. His people used to live in Granny's house—Tramore—but they're all dead."

To his great relief he saw that his words suggested nothing to Pascoe beyond their literal meaning. Indeed, Pascoe seemed disappointed. "I don't see why you couldn't have said so at once, then," he grumbled, "instead of making a mystery about it. As it happens, people when they die *don't* become angels. Angels are quite different; they've never been human. So if the window has a picture of an angel, it only means that they hope this boy has gone to heaven."

He paused for a moment, and then pursued cynically: "Everybody when they die is supposed by their relations to go to heaven. . . . If you were to judge by all the stuff you read on tombstones you'd think the other place didn't exist."

For Tom it didn't, or rather it didn't interest him, his conception of it being so narrowly cut and dried as to discourage all imaginative speculation, whereas heaven was simply crammed with possibilities. "Do you think there'll be animals there?" he asked, and to his surprise Pascoe, who rarely laughed, gave an odd little chuckle.

"In heaven? Since Roger came from there, I suppose he'll go back again. . . . Which means," he went on, "that you'll have to be jolly careful if you want to be with him instead of with Barker and Pincher."

It was the first joke Tom had ever known him to make, but, though he thought it quite a good one, he pursued his own fancy. "Mother does. . . . She thinks there will be animals for people who wouldn't be happy without them. And the sea will be there for the same reason—for people who are fond of it. . . . Stop!"

The last word was really a cry of alarm, called forth because Pascoe, with the end of a branch, had suddenly begun to poke among the withered leaves gathered in a hole, and Tom knew what else was there. But his warning came too late. Like the imprisoned jinn in the *Arabian Nights* story, a cloud of bees seemed literally to *flow* out, and next moment the air was filled with their angry buzzing. It was no time for hesitation, and Tom and Pascoe took to their heels. Down into the glen they plunged, down the bank and across the stream. Up the other bank—tripping, slipping, and stumbling—trying to beat off their savage assailants, and above all to shield their faces—while Roger barked and raced on ahead. It was not on him, it was on the two boys, that punishment was falling. Utterly reckless of their own lives so long as they could plant a sting somewhere in the enemy, the bees pursued them to the very hall door, and even as Tom slammed it behind him he could see a bee crawling in Pascoe's hair, and feel one or two who must have got down his own back and beneath his shirt. "Come on!" he cried. "We'll have to take off all our clothes. I'm stung in about sixty different places, and there are some still walking about, I can feel them."

Nor had he greatly exaggerated. Up in his bedroom, when they had pulled off their shirts and turned them inside out, they found several bees still alive. Now that the attack was over, Tom began to laugh, but Pascoe seemed not far from weeping, for though both were about equally stung the effect upon him had been much more severe. Upon Tom it had been no more than the stabbing of a number of little red-hot needles; the pain, though sharp, was superficial. Pascoe, on the contrary, where the stings had entered was already beginning to swell up in surprising little lumps, so that Tom, alarmed by the spectacle presented, opened the door and shouted for Mother.

"Wait!—wait!" Pascoe cried irritably. "Wait, can't you, till I get on my trousers!"

"Wait!" Tom echoed, for Mother was by now half-way upstairs. She must have heard the clamour in the hall, and from broken phrases and exclamations have guessed what had happened. Holding the door very slightly ajar, Tom kept her outside on the landing while he explained the situation. "Have you got them on yet?" he called back over his shoulder, and a muffled affirmative being returned, Mother was then permitted to enter and administer first aid.

Pascoe, trousered indeed, but otherwise unclothed, lay face downward on the bed, and there was no doubt he was pretty badly stung. Having done all she could, Mother finally suggested that he might like to go home—a remark which, more than any of the remedies she had brought with her, had an excellent effect both as stimulant and restorative. Pascoe didn't want to go home. He very rightly didn't see what good missing all the fun was going to do his stings, so Mother hastened to reassure him. It was only that she thought he must be feeling very sore and uncomfortable, in spite of the splendid way he had taken it—making so little fuss, when most people would have been moaning and groaning.

"He's like the Spartan boy and the fox," Tom put in, paying his tribute, and these timely blandishments clearly brought their measure of consolation.

Lunch revived the Spartan boy still further, for, as Tom had expected, he proved to be exactly the kind of boy Daddy liked, and the appreciation was mutual. The meal concluded, they waited till Mother was ready, and then all four set out to walk to the field. Daddy had suggested driving, but Mother had thought not, as there was bound to be a crowd, quite apart from the procession. "Poor creatures!" she sympathized, "beating those big drums and carrying enormous banners on a day like this! They'll be utterly exhausted, and the field will be like a fiery furnace, with not even a tree to give the slightest shade!"

"The greater the discomfort the greater the glory," Daddy reminded her. "Also, a certain amount of refreshment, I imagine, will be produced from hip-pockets."

This, so far as Mother was concerned, was an unfortunate suggestion. "I hope not," she murmured doubtfully. "I'm relying on what Mr. Sabine said—that every year sees an improvement in that direction."

More by good luck than calculation, they had timed their departure accurately, for the shrill sound of fifes, soaring above the deep roll and pounding of drums, was already audible in the distance when they emerged on to the main road. Mother and Daddy hurried on, in order to reach the field before the procession, while Tom and Pascoe, who wished to watch it passing, climbed on to a bank.

And here it was—the first banners swinging and dipping round the bend of the road, brilliantly purple and orange in the sunlight. At the same moment the leading band, which had been marking time by heavy drum-beats, suddenly burst into its own particular tune, and Tom, carried away on the wings of the infectious rhythm, raised his voice in song:

Sit down, *my pink and* be *content,*
For the cows are in the clover.

They were the words he had learned from James-Arthur, and whether right or wrong they fitted into the tune; but Pascoe, less excited, nudged him violently in the ribs to show him he was attracting attention. All the same, it *was* exciting—each band playing its special tune, which, as the players drew closer, disentangled itself from all the other tunes, till it became for a minute or two the only one, and then, passing on into the distance, was itself lost in the next and the next and the next—a constant succession. The big drums, crowned with bunches of orange lilies, were splotched and stained with blood from the hands of the drummers, whose crimson faces streamed with sweat. . . . It was great! Flags waved; musical instruments gleamed and glittered; the drums pounded; the fifes screamed! Yet in the midst of all this strident Dionysiac din and colour, the men and boys carrying the great square banners, or simply marching in time to the music, looked extraordinarily grave. It was only the accompanying rag tag and bobtail who exhibited signs of levity, bandied humorous remarks, and threw orange-skins—the actual performers were rapt in the parts they were playing in a glorious demonstration, which, if secular, had nevertheless all the bellicose zeal and earnestness of a declaration of faith. The very pictures on the banners were symbols of that faith. "The Secret of England's Greatness"—in other words, Queen Victoria presenting Bibles to kneeling blackamoors, passionately grateful to receive them—was a subject second in popularity only to King William himself. It told a story, it expressed an ideal—or if not an ideal at any rate an immovable conviction. . . . And there, marching along and helping to carry a banner, was the other, the more familiar William, yet not quite the William of every day. Tom screamed his name at the top of his voice, but William, who must have heard, took no notice.

"Don't!" Pascoe said, glancing uneasily to right and left.

"Don't what?" answered Tom impatiently.

"You're dancing up and down: everybody's staring at you."

This was purely a figment of imagination, for nobody was paying the least attention to them, but Pascoe seemed to have a morbid dread of publicity.

The procession took nearly three hours to pass, and they waited till the end before themselves adjourning to the field. There the speeches had begun, but they were not interested in these. They wandered through the crowd; they listened to Mr. Sabine for a few minutes; they saw Max and avoided him; and they had begun to feel that the best of the show was over when Tom's arm was grabbed from behind. "We've been looking for you," Mother said. "Daddy and I are going home and you'd both better come with us: I'm sure you've had enough of all this; *I* certainly have. Besides, you must be hungry; we had lunch so early."

It was what they had been thinking themselves, so they complied at once, and began to thread their way through the crowd, Daddy and Pascoe leading, Tom following with Mother.

"Did you see James-Arthur?" he questioned eagerly. "He's with his girl."

"What girl?" Mother answered. "And don't talk like that."

"Like what?" Tom said; and then: "Why?"

"Because I don't like it—especially coming from a little boy."

"Well—anyhow she's Nancy from the Green Lion."

Mother laughed. "Such nonsense! I suppose she was asking him how he was enjoying himself. Nancy used to be the Sabines' maid, and I should think must be old enough to be James-Arthur's mother."

CHAPTER XVII

"I wonder how long this is going to last?" Mother said, pausing with the coffee-pot in her hand, but addressing nobody in particular, as she gazed out next morning through streaming window-panes at the soaked and dripping garden. "I should have thought it might have rained itself out by now: twice I woke up in the night and it was coming down in a deluge. It's extraordinary the luck they always have for their procession. Just imagine if it had been like this yesterday!"

Tom imagined it, and Daddy said: "The rain will do a lot of good: in fact if it keeps on all day I shan't be sorry; the garden needs it. . . . Unfortunately the glass seems to be on the turn again."

He got up as he spoke to give it a further tap, which suggested to Tom how much better an arrangement it would be if the barometer affected the weather instead of the weather the barometer. "Then we could fix it so that it would never rain except at night."

"Wouldn't that be rather unfair to some of your nocturnal friends?" Daddy reminded him, and after a prolonged and impartial consideration Tom was afraid it would.

Supposing such an alteration could be made, Alfred for one wouldn't like it. Nor would the owls who lived at Denny's, nor the rats who lived by the river. Perhaps, then, things were better as they were. Yet it was an interesting question, and he began to ruminate on how his proposed amendment would go if put to the vote in a parliament of beasts. Cows and horses and dogs would vote for it, and of course wasps, bees, and butterflies; but frogs and ducks probably would vote on the other side, and cats and bats certainly would. Field mice would be for, and possibly indoor mice against. As he kept on enumerating the ayes and the noes he was impressed by the diversity of taste among Earth's children, and the wonderful impartiality with which she looked after them all. She had no favourites—as he feared in her place he would have had—a hippopotamus, a blackbird, and a boy were equally pleasing to her, equally provided for, equally her sons. From which it most clearly followed that none had a right to interfere with or rob the others of *their* rights.

Having discovered this truth, he immediately tried to communicate it, and was surprised when Mother told him he would find it expressed in the very first chapter of Genesis, when the various creatures are brought to Adam that he may name them: but Daddy, whose gaze had been fixed upon him throughout his struggle to find the right words, here interposed. "I don't think that's quite what he means:"—and on Tom's confirming head-shake—"it goes further than that. The Edenic doctrine is autocratic, whereas Tom's is based on an ethical conception of the greater democracy."

"I'm afraid I don't know what the greater democracy is," Mother said.

Daddy knew, however; and though from his choice of such long words Tom suspected that he was not taking it seriously,

and breathed into his mouth-organ. If it had not been for his so lachrymose appearance Tom might have suspected this strange old man of mocking him, but his tearful eyes had far too melancholy an expression for that, and even his long nose was mournful. His grey hair, too, was long and thin and dank, and hung straight down like his drooping hands, which seemed all pendulous fingers. But his wavering shape was growing ever more uncertain and transparent, fainter and fainter, till suddenly a golden shaft pierced him through, and without even a sigh he vanished. His world was vanishing also—curling up, evaporating—as if the sun were a dragon and had put forth a great fiery tongue that wound about it, lapping it up, and leaving only at the edges a few diminishing wisps of white drifting vapour.

When it was quite gone, Tom descended the ladder and came round to the garden, which he found transformed, like some garden in an Arabian tale after a shower of precious stones. Everything was soaking wet, and from each leaf and blade of grass the light in all the colours of the spectrum was refracted as through a prism. He gazed up at the sun between nearly closed fingers, because an angel lived there. The angel's name was Uriel, but Tom had never been able to discover him, and he did not see him now. Roger found him thus engaged, and soon afterwards Pascoe arrived—both very wet, for Roger had come across the fields and through the glen, and Pascoe must have left home while it was still raining.

The latter looked uncomfortably hot, which was not surprising, seeing that he was encased in a sort of shining black cocoon, composed of waterproof trousers, cape, and hat. "I wish I'd waited till it was fine," he grumbled, wheeling his bicycle into the porch. "These beastly things may keep out the rain, but they make you nearly as wet as if they didn't: my shirt's sticking to me."

"What's in the parcel?" Tom inquired, glancing curiously at a brown-paper parcel, oblong in shape and of considerable size, which was fastened to the carrier of the bicycle.

Pascoe unstrapped it. "It's things for making a kite," he

said—"just some laths and linen. I didn't know it was going to clear up, so I thought we might as well make a kite."

Tom had never possessed, nor even seen a kite, and he thought Pascoe's plan a good one, though it had a drawback. "What about Roger?" he said. "I mean, if we're going to work all morning up in the loft, he'll find it very dull, and he can't get up by the foot-board. . . . I've tried carrying him, but it's no use; he struggles like mad and he's frightfully strong."

Pascoe frowned. This perpetual fuss about Roger seemed to him exaggerated, and in any case a nuisance. He liked dogs himself, but he liked them sensibly. What is more, he was convinced that if Roger had been a human being Tom would have shown no such compunction about leaving him. Nevertheless, he considered the problem, while they walked round to the yard.

Beneath the loft he paused thoughtfully, gazing up at the window before entering the motor-house. Here he paused again. "We ought to be able to arrange something," he murmured, while Tom, who had the greatest confidence in his friend's practical ingenuity and inventiveness, said "Yes," and waited expectantly.

"It'll have to be a lift," Pascoe deliberated, "but that shouldn't be difficult; and the best place to put it would be exactly under the trap-door, so that the foot-board will help to keep it from tilting."

"He'd jump out," Tom said.

"Well, that's his look-out. All the same, I bet if he's really anxious he'll soon pick up the idea, and one of us can stand below for the first trip or two. After all, he's a sheep-dog, and you can teach a sheep-dog anything. . . . Where's William?"

"William!" Tom repeated. "What do you want William for?"

"I don't. It's just that to do the thing properly we ought to have a winch or something, for the rope to go round."

Tom was less ambitious. "We can pull him up without a winch," he said; for he could see that Pascoe presently would be wanting a bell for Roger to ring. "Anyhow, William's not here; he's recovering from yesterday."

This, as he knew, was a gratuitous libel on that strictest of teetotallers, but Pascoe, who had begun to hunt among a pile of wooden boxes and cases, was too busy to notice it. Very soon he found what he thought might do, and dragged it out. "There's just about room for him if we take off the lid and knock out the partitions; and it's got handles we can tie the ropes to. As a matter of fact it's an old wine case, which is why it's so well made."

Tom was dubious. "He'd never stay in that, and if he jumped out when it was half-way up he might hurt himself. Dogs' legs are very easily hurt; they're different from cats'."

"Just as you like," Pascoe replied. "I believe he'd be all right, but if you're nervous we'd better wait till we can get a basket or something we can shut him into. . . . Only," he added, "if we're going to make the kite this morning, we'll have to begin soon."

"Of course we'll make it," Tom gave in. "Roger'll have to stay down in the yard."

This was all Pascoe wanted, and he lifted his parcel. "If you can borrow a pair of scissors for cutting out the linen," he said, "I think I have everything else."

"Won't you need paste? There's a tube of seccotine in my tool-box, but seccotine makes your fingers stick to everything."

"I'm going to use nails," Pascoe said. "I brought some with me—specially small ones. My father has a workshop, you know."

Tom didn't know, but it now appeared that Pascoe's father was an expert carpenter. "He made a lovely cabinet for Mother's birthday, and the drawers slip in and out as smoothly as if they were sliding on butter. He says himself that that's the best test of good workmanship: in cheap modern furniture the drawers never work properly. . . . When you're getting the scissors, get some old newspapers and string too. You may as well be making the tail while I'm making the kite."

Tom departed on these errands, and when he returned Pascoe was already up in the loft, where he had cleared the table and unpacked his materials. Tom watched him for a minute or two, as he laid out and secured the framework of the kite; then, Pascoe having shown him what to do, he himself set to work on the tail, cutting the newspaper into strips and rolling these into solid wedges, which he knotted at regular intervals on the cord.

"Make them thick," Pascoe warned him, "and it'll need plenty. If the tail isn't heavy enough the kite won't fly steadily, but dive about all over the place, and very likely get smashed on the ground."

"I know—I know," Tom muttered, for if making the tail was not difficult, neither was it particularly interesting—all the interesting work was being done by Pascoe, who having completed the frame and laid it on the tightly-stretched linen, was now drawing on this the shape to be cut out. He seemed to be quite as good at making kites, Tom thought, as he had been at making the aquarium; clearly the example, or the lessons of Pascoe senior had not been thrown away. But he must have a special gift as well—inherited very likely—just as *he*, according to Mother and Doctor Macrory, took after Uncle Stephen. In that case, he suspected, Uncle Stephen wasn't a carpenter. Nor was Daddy, who couldn't be trusted even to fix a blind, Mother said, without making it ten times worse than it had been before. . . . All the same, he would have liked to know rather more particularly just in what way he *did* take after Uncle Stephen. Nobody had explained this, and Granny seemed to think it was all nonsense. Tom didn't believe it was nonsense, and felt extremely curious about Uncle Stephen—though there wasn't much chance of his curiosity ever being gratified, unless by some miracle Uncle Stephen should become curious about *him*. . . .

These reflections were interrupted by Pascoe, who without looking up from his work suddenly asked; "Did I tell you I saw Max on the road?"

"No," Tom answered, in a tone which indicated he had no desire to pursue the subject.

"Well, I did," Pascoe said, "and he had his gun. Imagine going out shooting on a morning like that—though of course it was clearing up by then. . . . I'm going to use seccotine after all—just to finish things off."

Tom took this as a signal that he might get up to inspect the progress he had made. It was a big kite Pascoe had designed—about three feet by two. "The square ones are the best," he said. "The others may look more ornamental, but they never fly so well."

"*I* think it looks great!" Tom declared.

So perhaps did Pascoe, though he replied modestly that it was too soon to judge. "Wait till we see how she goes. It all depends on the balance—and the belly-band may have to be altered, though I *think* it's all right."

"Will we be able to fly it this afternoon?" Tom asked.

"Not unless you buck up with the tail. You're taking a deucy long time over it."

But this Tom took to be merely a cautionary remark: he was pretty sure that Pascoe had every intention of flying the kite that afternoon, and during lunch the conversation was devoted exclusively to his and Daddy's earlier flyings. Daddy thought that Chinese boys had kites shaped like boxes, which didn't require tails, but he was unable to tell Pascoe where he could find a description of how to make one. He admired *their* kite, and so did Mother and Phemie and Mary, to all of whom Tom displayed it, while Pascoe remained quietly in the background.

The best place for a trial, they decided, would be Denny's fields, where they could get an open space without trees. So they set out, still chattering eagerly as sparrows about the kite, and taking it in turns to carry it. "You can try it first," Pascoe said, which—seeing that it was he who had thought of it, and made it, and supplied all the materials, including a ball of whipcord—was jolly decent of him. On their way they came upon James-Arthur: and James-Arthur, forsaking a cart he was loading with turnips, joined them to witness the start. Roger and Barker of course were there; but Pincher wasn't: ever since Max's advent Pincher had become an infrequent visitor, though he came as often as he could escape.

Pascoe now held up the kite and instructed Tom what to do.

"Run as hard as you can against the wind, and we'll soon see if she's all right."

She was. A fair wind was blowing down the field, and as Tom ran into it the kite rose behind him, and once it had reached a certain height did all the rest itself. It rose nearly straight, and as rapidly as he could let out the cord. Then, each in turn held it, so as to judge of the strength of its pull. The only disappointing thing was that neither Roger nor Barker showed the slightest interest—indeed actually turned their backs and looked the other way: Pincher would at least have barked. . . .

Presently it was so high up that it floated against the sky like a seagull. It could mount no higher now unless it broke free, for the cord had run out. So Tom and Pascoe sat down on the damp grass and gazed up at it, while James-Arthur returned to his work.

"I bet Roger or Barker couldn't hold it: I bet it would pull them up."

"Of course. I bet it would pull up even a small boy; or if it didn't, at any rate he'd have to let it go."

"Let's send up messengers," Pascoe said.

He straightway produced a dozen messengers from his pocket, evidently prepared beforehand, for they were circular discs of thick white paper with a nick cut at the side so that they could be slipped over the string. It was the strangest thing, for the messengers, caught by the wind, rose right up till they reached the kite itself, yet they wouldn't fly up at all if you just flung them loose into the air. Tom had never before even heard of messengers, and asked Pascoe if he had invented them. But he hadn't, and thought probably it was Chinese boys who had. The messengers were better fun than the kite itself, but they were quickly exhausted. After that, just holding the string became rather a bore, so they crossed the field and tied it to the top bar of a gate, while they played, for lack of anything better, a game of cocks and hens.

"I suppose that's why kites went out of fashion," Pascoe presently remarked.

"Why?"

"Because there's nothing more to do once they're up in the air. Daddy says all the boys flew them when he was a boy; and there was a particular season for them, and for tops and marbles. But none of the boys have them now. Even James-Arthur had never seen one."

"Neither had I—except in a picture."

"That's what I mean. They're not much use really, except for the sport of making them. I wonder where I could find out how to make a box-kite?"

"They're as good as boats anyway," Tom declared. "There's nothing to do with them either, except watch them."

Pascoe agreed. "It was really Daddy who wanted me to make a kite—I expect just because he used to fly them himself. The first time I made one he helped me with it. . . . Here's your father, too; come out specially, I suppose, because *he* used to have one."

It was true, for there he was, approaching from the far end of the meadow, which at any ordinary time would have been a most unlikely place for him to take a walk. Pascoe's brow was puckered slightly, and he said slowly; "I wonder what they'd do if they were left all alone with tops and marbles, and it was the proper season. . . . I mean, if there was nobody to watch them. I bet they'd play, if they were sure no one would ever hear about it."

"I don't believe Daddy would," Tom answered loyally.

"Not even if it was the season?" Pascoe murmured, which made Tom glance at him suspiciously; but Daddy had already hailed them, and they ran to meet him.

CHAPTER XVIII

Tom wished Pascoe would come home again. He had been away now for over a fortnight, staying at the seaside with some aunt or other who lived in Donegal, and a picture-postcard received that morning, mentioning that he was bathing every day, and hoping Tom was well, said not a word about when he expected to return. Also there was another reason why Tom had found the postcard unsatisfactory. Pascoe had been so very particular about leaving his address and getting him to promise to write (which he *had* done, quite a long letter, all four pages of a sheet of notepaper), yet this brief scrawl was the sole communication he had got in reply—nine words, two of which were Pascoe's name.

He wouldn't have minded this had he only sent a postcard himself—which was all he would have sent had not Pascoe made such a fuss about letters. But he had not only made the fuss, he had even invented a special cipher in which the letters were to be written, so that if they fell into the wrong hands they would be unreadable by anyone who didn't know the code. And the cipher was so extremely complicated that even with the code before him it had taken Tom hours to write his first page. After that, he had abandoned it; and Pascoe hadn't bothered to use it at all. . . .

Another and much queerer thing was that he had wanted Tom to make a compact by which they should solemnly bind themselves by a "blood oath" to continue to be chums after school recommenced. Tom had said of course they would continue, but he hadn't seen any necessity for the shedding of blood. Why, he had asked, should school make a difference? Pascoe, however, seemed to think it might, and this distrustful attitude had struck Tom as very strange until it occurred to him that Pascoe appeared to have made no friends at his previous school. He had gathered this in the first days of their acquaintance—not just from Brown's remarks, which probably were prejudiced—but from one or two let drop by Pascoe himself, though these had made little impression at the time, and later had been forgotten. The "blood compact" reminded him. It was as if Pascoe feared Tom might find somebody at school he would prefer for a special chum, though how a compact was to prevent this was hard to understand. In point of fact Tom already knew somebody he would have preferred—James-Arthur—but naturally he kept this to himself, nor could he see how it made the slightest difference in his friendship with Pascoe, which was of another and more practical kind, consisting largely in doing things together, or making things—like the kite and the aquarium—for Pascoe took no interest in ordinary regulation games such as tennis or croquet. After one or two unsuccessful trials, Tom had abandoned these as hopeless; but there was no doubt, though he might be a dud at orthodox games, Pascoe was jolly good at planning unorthodox ones—or rather schemes—and at carrying them out. So it was not surprising that in his absence Tom should miss him, and find himself now and then at a loose end. Occasionally he played a game of croquet or tennis with Mother; and every day with Roger and Barker he went over to Denny's on the very improbable chance of finding James-Arthur doing something at which he could help; but this was all. . . .

By far the best of these days had been that of the mowing of the great meadow, when in the evening he had ridden back to the farmhouse on Apollo, one of the solemn old carthorses. True, Apollo was so big, or else so preoccupied with private meditations, that he never seemed to know whether Tom was on his back or not, but pursued his way, or halted to sample some attractive specimen of vegetation, just as it pleased him. On this particular evening he had stopped to drink from a well, and in spite of coaxings and expostulations had drunk so much that he had got broader and broader till it was like balancing yourself on a cask. Tom, to be sure, may only have imagined this increase in bulk, for at no time were his legs long enough to obtain a proper grip, but the fact remained that when one of the men gave Apollo a playful smack with his open hand, and Apollo, surprised at this unexpected treatment, broke into a lumbering trot, Tom had slid gently off behind. Then everybody laughed, including James-Arthur, but they soon set him up again.

It had been a good day, and in the general atmosphere of rough friendliness he had felt very happy. He had eaten his supper that evening in Denny's kitchen, and afterwards walked home with James-Arthur. "Would you like me to fetch the owl?" James-Arthur had asked. "Just you watch and I'll bring him in a minute."

They paused in the deepening twilight by some beech-trees, and now James-Arthur locked his hands together and blew between his upright thumbs, producing a "Hoo, hoo, hoo, hoo, hoo!" He next mimicked the squeak of a mouse—once, twice, thrice—at irregular intervals—and soon after, sure enough, there was the owl, floating soundless as a ghost above their heads.

"You can always bring him," said James-Arthur, "but he won't stay when he sees it's only us."

Tom was filled with admiration, for this was far better than any artificial bird-call, and James-Arthur promised to teach him how to do it. They walked on, while the moon, large as a harvest moon, rose up over the trees and threw their shadows and the shadows of the trees on the silvered grass. James-Arthur had his arm round Tom's shoulder. He often walked like this, though only when there was nobody else there. Yet in spite of the intimacy thus created, he always called him "Master Tom", never just Tom, which would have shown that they were really chums and was what Tom would have liked.

CHAPTER XIX

One morning, a few days after the arrival of Pascoe's postcard, he was in the garden stretched full length on the grass in what to most people would have seemed an extremely uncomfortable position for reading; nevertheless Tom was reading, and with profound interest, a work Doctor Macrory had lent him. This was *The Library* of Apollodorus, and Mother, who had glanced through it, thought it a most extraordinary choice on the doctor's part. In some amusement she had turned the leaves of the two learned-looking volumes, with their Greek text printed on one page, and Sir James Frazer's English translation on the page opposite. Yet at the same time she could not help feeling pleased, for it showed that Doctor Macrory, who was a very intelligent man, must think Tom no ordinary little boy, and, since she certainly shared this opinion, she was content to leave the rest to be tested by experiment. As a matter of fact the doctor had made no mistake: the tales Apollodorus had to tell of Greek gods and heroes, though he boiled them down to their bare bones, as it were—presenting them without embellishment, and in the somewhat sparse and dry manner of an historian concerned only with plain facts and not at all with their imaginative treatment—Tom found as absorbing as those of Grimm or Asbjörnsen. More so, in a sense, because he could not help feeling that what had once been accepted as truth might *really* be true, or at any rate partly true; while as for the imaginative treatment, he could supply that himself. He supplied it, indeed, so lavishly, that though separated in time by nearly two thousand years, he and the ancient Greek mythologist became collaborators—a result all the more easily reached because Apollodorus made not the slightest attempt to criticize or explain his material. The only stumbling-block lay in the pronunciation of a good many unfamiliar names, and since Tom tackled these in the boldly sporting manner of Mr. Silas Wegg, it was a very minor one.

He had reached the story of the little boy Glaukos, who, while pursuing a mouse, fell into a jar of honey and was drowned (though a little later restored to life by a medicinal herb brought by a kindly serpent), when suddenly he heard a low whistle, and glancing up, saw James-Arthur at the gate. He was surprised, for James-Arthur had not often visited the house, and that he should come at such an hour, when naturally he ought to be working, made it more surprising still. James-Arthur waited at the gate, but he did not open it, so Tom jumped up and ran to see what he wanted. He was standing in the road, looking grave and rather troubled, and in his arms was a squirrel—a dead squirrel.

For a moment there was silence; then James-Arthur said: "I brought him, Master Tom: I thought maybe you'd wish to have him: he's yours—the one you made a pet of, that lived in the big oak-tree in the meadow. . . . Now he's dead. . . . Young Sabine shot him."

Tom had turned very white, and James-Arthur shuffled his feet and looked uncomfortable.

"I think maybe he didn't know he was yours," he went on, in a gruff, awkward attempt at consolation. Then abruptly and with a complete change of manner he added: "But he must have known he was tame, for you can see he shot him from quite close—dirty bastard! He was always that anyway."

Tom took the small body in silence. He looked down at it as it lay limply in his arms. The eyes were filmed and half closed, the little hands, once so quick to take nuts and cherries, were closed too, and a trickle of blood had smeared and matted the thick red fur.

"I thought maybe you'd wish to have him," said James-Arthur again; "so you could bury him in the garden."

"Thank you."

James-Arthur looked at him and did not seem to know what more to say. "I can't stop, Master Tom, for I have a cart waiting . . . but I'm sorry."

"Yes," said Tom. And after a pause he added; "I know you are."

He brought the body into the garden, holding it close to him. He kissed the soft fur and his face puckered, as if the tears he had kept back were on the point of falling. But suddenly a wave of furious anger swept through him. He carried Edward up to the loft and laid him gently on the table. For a minute or two he stood motionless, his face still white, but his mouth now firmly set; then he descended the ladder and set off for the Rectory.

He had no definite plan of action in view; certainly it was not Max he was in search of, for he knew he could do little or nothing even if he did meet him: nevertheless his mind was filled with hatred and the desire for revenge. Not that he believed an interview with Mr. Sabine would achieve anything. A few perfunctory words perhaps, and an expression of regret, but that would be all; he had no expectation that Max would be punished. The first momentary thought of getting James-Arthur to give him what he deserved he had abandoned also, for that would only be to create trouble for James-Arthur himself—possibly serious trouble, both for him and his mother, if Mr. Sabine took the matter up, as he would be sure to do. Tom didn't know much about Mr. Sabine, but he knew the gun had come from him—Max himself had told Pascoe so—and that he approved of his shooting.

Uncertain what he should do, yet his mind seething with passion, he hurried along, meeting nobody on the road; and when he reached the Rectory and rang the bell it was Miss Sabine he asked for. The maid—Phemie's and Mary's friend—invited him to come in, because Miss Sabine was busy in the kitchen making jam, and he might have to wait for a minute or two. Tom muttered that he would wait where he was. He had heard Althea's voice in the distance, and did not wish to talk to her just now. Besides, in the brief space occupied by this exchange of words, he had caught sight of Max's gun leaning against the hat stand, where it had evidently been left temporarily; and in a flash he had made up his mind. The maid departed to tell Miss Sabine he was there, and five seconds later Tom was scudding down the garden path and along the road, with the gun in his hand.

He made directly for the river, and once or twice glanced back over his shoulder, but nobody was following. Nevertheless it was not till he had reached the tow-path that he paused to draw breath. He stood motionless now, with the gun in his hands, as if for the first time he had begun to realize what he had done, and what it must lead to. The moment the gun was missed, though this might not be till Max himself missed it, the whole thing would be clear to everybody. That, however, did not matter, was indeed just as he would have wished, for the secret destruction of the gun would somehow have been nothing. He lifted it by the barrel and brought it down with all his force on the path; but either the ground was too soft, or he was not strong enough, for it did not break, nor did he try again, but flung it out into the middle of the river, where, with a splash, it sank.

Tom stood watching the ripples spreading out in a widening circle, yet feeling no relief beyond a momentary satisfaction.

What he had done was useless, altered nothing, could not bring Edward back to life. It was a poor kind of revenge too; but the right kind, which would have been to fight Max and hammer him till he sobbed and begged for mercy, was beyond his power. Walking back to his own house, he felt more and more depressed. Nor could he now tell anybody—not even Mother—to whom he naturally would have gone for sympathy. He had an impulse to seek out James-Arthur and tell *him*, for he would know at once from James-Arthur's manner whether he thought what he had done a rotten as well as a futile thing; and by the time he had reached home and climbed up once more to the loft, he had begun to wish he had not done it, and then again to be glad he *had* done it. He cried a little as he stroked Edward's soft fur and placed his body in a box—with a straw bed for it to lie on—and presently took the box down and buried it in the shrubbery. He marked the spot where he would put up a stone with Edward's name on it when Pascoe came back. Edward was nothing to Pascoe; Pascoe had never even seen him: but he would help, and make everything neat and orderly—and more than ever, Tom, in his unhappiness, wished he was there now.

CHAPTER XX

During lunch he was so silent that Daddy asked him what was the matter. He returned the answer usually given in these circumstances, but he could see that, whatever Daddy might think of it, it did not convince Mother. She kept on glancing at him, and in the end asked him if he had a headache. Why a headache? Tom wondered gloomily, but he tried to look more animated. He was quite well, he repeated, yet, though Mother did not press him further, he knew this was only because Daddy was there, and not because she was satisfied. To set him at his ease she began to talk of other things—chiefly of the visitors she was expecting for tea that afternoon. Tom listened with a wandering attention. He could have informed her that he too was expecting a visitor—but one who probably would inquire for Daddy. . . .

He escaped as soon as he could, seizing the opportunity while Mother was giving directions to Mary, and ran out into the garden, where, like Adam and Eve, he took refuge in the shrubbery. Here before long he was discovered by Roger, who with his usual cleverness grasped the situation at once, and here they both skulked out of sight, while keeping a sharp watch on the approach to the house.

The visitor Tom was expecting would arrive, he was sure, long before Mother's friends; and of course it might be only Max, in which case Tom would immediately come out into the open. On the other hand, it was far more likely to be Mr. Sabine. Max was bound to know—for, if he hadn't known before, James-Arthur would certainly have told him—that the squirrel he had murdered was Tom's pet; and he would guess from this at least part of the truth, and tell the rest of his family—particularly his father. Well—let him! Tom didn't care. Only he wished that whatever was going to happen would happen soon. . . .

Very likely Miss Sabine was one of the visitors Mother had invited to her tea-party, but *she* would say nothing; at any rate not till she got Mother alone. For that matter, Miss Sabine might even be on his side—to some extent at least—certainly it wouldn't be for love of Max if she wasn't. Mother might too—he wasn't sure—but Daddy he felt certain wouldn't. . . .

Roger was very quiet, evidently perfectly content to sit like this, with Tom's arm round him, as they had sat so often before. Roger had beautiful brown eyes, very loving and trustful. Roger was thinking mysterious doggy thoughts, and he sat bolt upright, in which position his head was exactly on a level with Tom's own. . . .

They had been waiting now for nearly an hour, he supposed—which was strange surely, since Mr. Sabine's object, if he *were* coming, would be to catch Daddy before he went out. It began to look as if after all nobody were coming, and cautiously Tom ventured forth from his hiding-place, and stood thinking. Perhaps he ought to take just one peep down the road before going over to Denny's to consult with James-Arthur. But at the very moment of reaching this decision he saw the tall dark figure of Mr. Sabine at the gate, and for an instant they stood thus, face to face, not more than ten yards apart.

Mr. Sabine's hand was on the latch, but before he had spoken a word Tom turned tail and fled back into the shrubbery, and from the shrubbery down into the glen. It was hardly the behaviour of a hero, nor was it calculated to placate Mr. Sabine, whose voice could be heard in the distance calling after him. Tom, however, was already scrambling down the steep bank of the glen and had no intention of obeying the summons. What he had anticipated had happened, and oddly enough in a way he felt glad, for he knew that everything would now come out, so that when he returned to the house he would at least know what to expect. . . .

He clambered out of the glen and pursued his course straight across country. He had no idea where James-Arthur was or what he would be doing, but leaving the matter to Roger, very soon he found him digging potatoes in a field, and luckily he was alone.

Tom began at once, and James-Arthur, the sun streaming down on his flaxen head and open blue shirt and bare arms, stood motionless, leaning on his fork, while the story was poured out. As it proceeded, Tom from time to time glanced at him anxiously, but James-Arthur kept his eyes fixed on the ground, and it was impossible while he did so to guess what was passing in his mind. He did not speak once until Tom reached the point where he had thrown the gun into the river, and then he only said: "It's a pity you done that, Master Tom."

Tom stopped abruptly. "Why? Why is it a pity? I'm very glad I did. It's what he deserved."

"It is," returned James-Arthur laconically.

"Then why is it a pity? I don't see any pity about it."

James-Arthur spat on his hands, which were broad and powerful, and plunged his fork energetically into the ground. But it was a solitary plunge; he left it there; and proceeded to wipe his hands on his dirty corduroys. "It'll maybe get you into bad trouble if they find out," he answered.

"They've found out already," Tom told him. "Mr. Sabine was going up to the house when I left."

James-Arthur scratched his head in silence, and Tom immediately said: "Don't; your hands are all earthy." But this was involuntary, and because James-Arthur's hair was exactly the colour of very ripe oats, and looked as if it would show the slightest mark: next moment he returned to the matter he had come about. "Did you tell Max it was my squirrel?" he asked.

"I did, an' I told him how much you valued it, an' what I thought of him. But sure he had it destroyed before ever I come up. . . . It was the shot that brought me."

"What ought I to do now?"

James-Arthur scratched his head again, till remembering Tom's expostulation, he smiled sheepishly. The little boy's admiration had always puzzled and amused him, though it pleased him too. "You wouldn't go back—would you?" he suggested after a pause.

Tom was surprised. "Back where?"

"Back to your own house. . . . I mean before Mr. Sabine's gone. . . . It's just so they wouldn't think you might be hiding."

Since hiding was precisely what he *was* doing, Tom couldn't quite grasp the point of this remark. "You mean they'll think—Mr. Sabine will think—I'm frightened of him?"

"Aye," said James-Arthur slowly: "if he seen you, it'd maybe look like that."

Tom hung his head and began to kick at a lump of earth. "Of course he saw me," he muttered, but said nothing further till he felt James-Arthur's arm slipping round his shoulder in the old way. This, for some mysterious reason, had the alarming effect of making him want to cry, and also, in return, to put his arms round James-Arthur; but fortunately he was able to quash both impulses, and presently to ask in his normal voice: "What do *you* think?"

"Well, it's only natural you'd be a bit scared," James-Arthur thought. "I wasn't meaning that. I was only meaning—if so be you could keep from showing it too much—to oul' Sabine anyways."

"I'm not scared of him," Tom answered. "It's not that. It's——"

"What is it, Master Tom?"

"It's because they'll want me to tell him I'm sorry—Daddy will—and I'm not going to. I hate Max and I'd kill him if I could."

James-Arthur shook his head reprovingly. "Now, now, that's foolish talk, for you wouldn't do no such thing—because you're not that sort, an' never will be. If you were, you wouldn't be sorrowing over a dead squirrel at this moment."

"I'd hurt him anyway," Tom said; "and badly too, so that he'd remember it for a long time. You don't believe me, because you think I'm soft."

"No," James-Arthur replied. "I think you're tough enough in plenty of ways—other ways—a heap tougher than young Sabine I dare say. But I think you're soft-hearted, because I've seen it."

"I'm not," Tom denied.

James-Arthur smiled. "I don't mean anything you wouldn't like," he said. "But anyways it wouldn't hurt you—would it?—just to say you're sorry. Whether you are or not, it's only two words, an' it might make a lot of difference—though I suppose the oul' lad'll be lookin' a new gun."

Strangely enough, until James-Arthur mentioned it, this thought had never entered Tom's head; but now he instantly saw that the first thing Daddy would do on learning the truth would be to offer to replace the gun. It was sickening, hateful, unfair. Max had done a rotten, cruel thing, and in return he would get a new gun and carry on just as before; while Edward, who had never harmed anybody or anything, would never again be able to peep down from the branches of his oak-tree, to gather and stow away his winter stores, to come down at the sound of his name, and sit on Tom's shoulder and be stroked and petted. . . .

When he raised his head it was to find James-Arthur looking

at him very kindly. "Now don't you be taking on so, Master Tom. I wish I'd hit that young scut a clout on the head myself, an' if you were a bit nearer his match I'd tell you to leather into him an' break his jaw. But the way it is, it'd be no good."

Tom said nothing, and James-Arthur went on consolingly: "Troubles happen, but in the latter end they pass. So if they ask you to, just you say you're sorry, an' in a day or two it'll all be forgotten."

Then Tom at last found words. "I *won't*," he replied, his mouth closing obstinately. "They can keep on and on, and punish me in any way they like, but I'll never tell either Mr. Sabine or Max that I'm sorry, and I'll never speak to Max again."

CHAPTER XXI

When he got home William was cutting the grass on the croquet-lawn—probably on purpose, so that he might pounce on him at once. "The master's been lookin' for you all roads," he called out sourly. "Ever since Mr. Sabine come."

Tom halted irresolutely. "Is Mr. Sabine still here?" he said.

"He is not then; they give you up. An' if you ask me, he wasn't lookin' too pleased eether when he left—whatever you may have bin doin' to the gentleman."

Without replying to this insinuation, Tom thrust his hands into his pockets and walked on, assuming an air of nonchalance he was far from feeling. Through the open drawing-room windows floated the sound of mingled feminine voices, telling him that Mother's tea-party was still in full swing.

He went straight to the study, but outside the door paused for nearly a minute before opening it. Daddy was writing at the big leather-covered table near the window, and at the sound of Tom's entrance he glanced up; then, seeing who it was, sighed and laid down his pen. To Tom's surprise he did not look angry—

merely rather bored at the interruption, and at the same time half amused.

"Won't you sit down?" he asked politely, as his son lingered uneasily by the door; and Tom, uncertain what to make of this most Daddyish reception, sat down in the nearest chair.

Daddy removed his glasses and inspected him for a moment or two without speaking. This accomplished, he pushed back his chair, sighed again, stretched his legs, and said in the resigned accents of one embarking on a tedious duty: "I presume you already know that I've had the pleasure of a visit from Mr. Sabine—and why. He mentioned your encounter, and also that at sight of him you ran away. . . . I, unfortunately, was not in a position to do so."

The last words may or may not have been intended to reach Tom, whose sharp ears nevertheless caught them. It certainly was a most unexpected beginning, and a little more hopefully he began to wonder what really could have happened. Daddy still did not enlighten him. "That was a very ill-mannered thing to do," he went on, "and I must add, not at all like you. Yet when I ventured to say so to Mr. Sabine, he not only assured me that you had seen him, but that he called after you several times, and you took no notice. Naturally he arrived here in a somewhat heated mood—which I hope may account for the suspicions he expressed—and still clings to, I'm afraid."

"Did he tell you Max had shot my squirrel?" Tom asked in a low voice. "He shot Edward."

Something woebegone in his attitude must have struck Daddy, for he dropped his semi-ironical tone and answered quickly and kindly; "Yes, he told me so; but that Max had no idea the squirrel was a pet of yours when he shot it—which I'm sure is true."

"I don't believe it's true," Tom burst out. "He knew he was tame anyhow, because he shot him from quite close. He's always shooting things, and Mr. Sabine allows him to."

Daddy waited a moment before going on. "You see, Tom, it's like this: very few people quite share your feelings about animals. It may be unfortunate, but it is inevitable, because we are all born with a limited number of sympathies only, and yours, in that direction, happen to be unusually strong. I did my best to explain to Mr. Sabine how you felt about such things, but it would have been very much better if you had been there yourself, instead of taking to your heels as if you had done something you were ashamed of."

Tom gazed at him half incredulously, for there was a note in his voice, as he uttered this very mild reproof, far more friendly than angry.

"You think I did right?" he stammered.

"I don't think you did right to run away—which never helps anything—but I certainly think you had a much more legitimate grievance than Mr. Sabine, and I told him so."

Tom drew a deep sigh and murmured, "Thank you, Daddy."

"So that when you return the gun, or tell Max where you hid it, I imagine the apologies will be on the other side. In fact, taking everything into consideration, I think it will be sufficient if we send it back by William—unless you actually wish to have an interview with our reverend friend."

Tom's face fell. In one second all his newborn confidence came toppling to the ground, and he saw that if Daddy had taken his part it was due to a complete misunderstanding. He believed Tom had taken the gun, but no more than that, as indeed might have been guessed from his remarks about Mr. Sabine's suspicions. "I can't return it," he whispered.

It was strange, but Daddy still seemed not to comprehend. He merely looked puzzled. "Why?—why can't you return it? I don't suppose you've hidden it in such an inaccessible place that you can't lay your hands on it."

"I threw it in the river," Tom said; and those few words sufficed to change everything.

It was not that even now Daddy looked angry; but what was worse, he looked profoundly disappointed.

"So Mr. Sabine was right after all!"

"Yes," Tom said.

There followed a silence, which seemed to last for hours before

Daddy spoke again. "That, I'm afraid, alters the position. Don't you think it was a rather spiteful revenge to take?"

Tom did not answer, and Daddy went on: "Stupid too—since you must have known I should have to replace the gun."

"I didn't," Tom broke in eagerly. "I mean, I didn't think of that till James-Arthur told me you would."

"And what else did James-Arthur tell you? What does he think of the whole performance, for I suppose you talked it over?"

Tom's eagerness died. "I think he—— I think he thinks the same as you."

"Did he say so?"

"No."

Daddy sat there, as if he were turning over this last response in his mind, though Tom had not intended it to convey more than a bare negation. "If," he began at last, and speaking less sternly—"if Max had shot the squirrel knowing it was yours, I shouldn't blame you perhaps—at all events not so much. But he didn't; he did it in ignorance; which makes all the difference. . . . Don't imagine I approve of what he did: on the contrary, I think he must be an unpleasant boy; but that is not the point, nor does it justify your action. At any rate, the fact remains that I parted with his father on far from cordial terms; with the result that now I shall have to take you over to the Rectory and we shall both have to apologize."

Tom had been staring at the carpet, but when Daddy paused he once more looked up. For a moment, though his lips moved, no words came. Then; "I won't," he brought out in a low but extremely stubborn voice. "I'll say I'm sorry to you—about having to buy a new gun—but I won't say it to either Mr. Sabine or Max."

It was his nervousness, no doubt, that made it sound so openly defiant. None the less, it *had* that sound, and Daddy, who hitherto had been leaning back in his chair carelessly twiddling an ivory paper-knife, suddenly sat up straight, and Tom saw that now at all events he was genuinely angry. "I can't take you over there this evening," he said coldly, "because it is Wednesday, and Mr. Sabine will be conducting the church service, and possibly have other business to see to afterwards; but I shall take you over to-morrow morning."

"I won't go," Tom repeated.

"You certainly *will*," Daddy answered. "And in the meantime you had better go to your room, and remain there till you have learned to speak more respectfully."

CHAPTER XXII

Tom left him without a word.

In his own room he sat down on the side of the bed to think things over. The situation was at any rate definite and clear, and in one respect he was perhaps glad to be condemned to solitary confinement, since somehow it made it easier for him to keep to his resolve. Possibly, therefore, it would have been more satisfactory still had he been followed and locked in, though of course it was none the less imprisonment because this formality had been neglected.

His broodings were interrupted by the sound of voices, and he went to the window to watch Mother's departing guests. A little later he heard Mother herself coming upstairs, and turned round expectantly, but she passed his door without even pausing, and went on into her own room. Did she not know, then, what had happened? Or had Daddy told her he was to be left to himself till he showed signs of penitence, and promised to do what he was told? Very likely nobody would be allowed to come near him—except perhaps to bring him food, for even Daddy would hardly try to starve him into compliance. If he did, it wouldn't succeed; and he pictured himself fainting with hunger yet still defiant. . . .

He stood listening, for Mother was moving about in her room, getting ready for dinner. He could have gone to her there, and it was not so much obedience to Daddy's orders as an odd kind of pride that prevented him. Presently the gong sounded and he heard her again passing his door, this time going downstairs.

Well, he could be equally determined, and somebody must come soon unless they *were* going to starve him—either Phemie or Mary—he hoped Phemie.

This hope at all events was realized, indeed more than realized, for shortly afterwards Phemie came in beaming, and with an air of being so completely on his side that for a moment he thought she was going to kiss him. She carried a tray, too, on which was not only an ordinary dinner, but what looked very like a special treat in the shape of macaroons, of which, as she well knew, he was particularly fond. Even in the midst of his troubles he could not help feeling gloomily tickled, for he strongly suspected the macaroons to be spoils pillaged from Mother's tea-party. This surmise, as he learned later, was correct. Connecting his disgrace with Mr. Sabine's visit, Phemie had formed her own view of the situation, and had expressed it openly and with vigour. "Shutting up the poor lamb all alone there!—just because of old Nosey Sabine! Him and his Orange sash, and a face would turn the milk inside a cow! I never could abide him, and I wonder the Master would be heeding his complaints—as like as not a pack of lies invented by his own brat!"

Phemie's championship was the more striking, because in ordinary circumstances she herself was by no means slow to point out Tom's faults and call him to order. At present you would think there had never been even a passing tiff between them, and that from infancy he had been the apple of her eye. She set down the tray on a small table, hoped he would enjoy his dinner, and noticeably made no allusion to the macaroons. "And if you want any more," she told him, "or anything else, just you ring the bell and eether Mary or me will answer it."

She had taken jolly good care he wouldn't want more! Tom thought, as he surveyed the ample repast provided; but he promised, and when he had finished his meal, took a book from his shelf and lay down on the bed.

It was no use, however: he found it impossible to fix his mind for more than a sentence or two on what he was reading, and by and by a sudden shower beating sharply against the pane took him once more to the window. Outside, the aspect had changed; a light breeze had sprung up and the sky was dappled with floating shreds of cloud. One very dark cloud, purple-black in colour, and in shape resembling a gigantic bird floating on wide-spread wings, was drifting towards the horizon. It was from that cloud the shower must have come, and Tom decided it was like a condor, though all he knew of condors was derived from a cheerful little lyric by his favourite poet:

Flapping from out their Condor wings
Invisible Woe!

But at the sound of the opening door poetry was forgotten, and he wheeled round, expecting to see Phemie again, come this time to clear the table. It was not Phemie, however; it was Mother; and unlike Phemie she looked very far from smiling, with the consequence that his first instinctive movement towards her was checked abruptly. At the same time a mood of obduracy, even of antagonism, which Phemie's friendliness had temporarily dispelled, was revived. Why need she look like that? After all, he had been guilty of nothing so very dreadful! And with his back to the window he stood watching her guardedly, waiting for her first words.

Mother's first words hardly sustained the impressive effect of her entrance, being not in the least what she had intended to say. This was due to the spectacle of the neglected dinner-things, which at once prompted the irresistible question, "Why hasn't Mary come to clear away?"

Tom said he didn't know, but his relief was immediate. With the quickness of perception common to small boys, he divined that if Mother really were taking his behaviour so much to heart her attention could hardly have been distracted by a dinner-tray. Therefore he permitted his own features to relax to something hovering on the verge of a smile, though he still remained where he was, and more or less on the defensive.

Meanwhile, since her distraction had been only momentary,

and the result of a strong natural objection both to untidiness in general and to Mary's habitual carelessness, Mother's face had reassumed its former expression. Or very nearly, for Tom was conscious of a subtle modification, as if she had decided to abandon severity and to try persuasion instead. "I came to tell you it is bedtime," she began, "and to ask you to promise to be a good boy and do what Daddy wishes."

It was mildness itself, and Tom's tongue flickered for a moment over his lips, for this was a kind of attack he found far more difficult to meet than either scoldings or reproaches. Nevertheless he steeled himself against it, and returned her gaze unwaveringly. "I'm afraid I can't do that," he said.

Why couldn't he? poor Mother seemed to wonder; for the very quietness of his reply stressed alarmingly its obstinacy, so that having looked in vain for some sign of yielding, she at last turned away. It was against Daddy's advice that she was here at all; he had strongly urged that in the meantime she should hold no communication with the offender; but men were so stupid, and, anyway, he had never understood Tom. "Why are you so headstrong?" she asked gently.

"I'm not; but I'm not going to tell lies."

Mother waited a moment before she tried again. "It wouldn't be a lie," she said. "It wouldn't mean——" But in fact she didn't quite know what it would or wouldn't mean—beyond the restoration of peace, since Daddy insisted on it. What weakened her position still further was that she herself felt very far from amicably disposed towards Mr. Sabine. If Daddy were angry with Tom and wished to punish him, she didn't see why he couldn't have given him a smacking and have done with it, instead of insisting on what to her own mind seemed a quite unnecessary apology to Mr. Sabine. Really it was Max who deserved the smacking—an odious boy, and the direct and sole cause of all the trouble. She used to think Miss Sabine was inclined to be hard on Max, but now she fully agreed with her, and his father was just as much, perhaps even more, to blame. How, at any rate, he could reconcile it either with his conscience or his position as a clergyman to encourage his son to go about shooting harmless squirrels, she couldn't imagine! She would never feel the same again towards Mr. Sabine. She had told Daddy so, and a great deal more; but Daddy had pointed out that Tom wasn't being punished for being kind to animals—as she seemed to imply—but for deliberate disobedience; and that to pass this over would be fatal, and the worst possible thing for Tom himself in the long run. Daddy had actually told her not to kiss him good night unless she found him penitent, and she was quite sure that the first question he would ask on her return would be whether she had done so or not. But Tom was as much her son as his—a great deal more so if it came to that—and really there were limits——

At this juncture she caught sight of the macaroons, which had been saved up to eat in bed. There they were now, beside the pillow, and it was just like his innocence, she thought, not to have tried to hide them—as Max no doubt would have done. The macaroons were Phemie's handiwork, she guessed, for the stupid Mary never would have ventured on anything so daring. Or so kind, she added—mentally registering a good mark to Phemie's credit, while at the same time deciding not to see the macaroons. She did kiss him, too; justifying this departure from Daddy's injunctions by telling him to say his prayers, and that she hoped in the morning he would be a better boy. . . .

One effect at least, if not the desired one, her visit produced; and this was to impress on Tom how difficult it was going to be to keep up his present line of conduct. In the morning the battle with Daddy would begin all over again. . . . That is to say, if he were still here in the morning. . . .

Slowly he removed his jacket and hung it over the back of a chair. If he were *not* here—if he were at Granny's for instance. . . . He put his jacket on again, and sitting down on the side of the bed began thoughtfully to nibble a macaroon. . . .

Dusk slowly gathered in the room while, little by little, his plan took shape. He need not go downstairs—which indeed would be risky on account of Mother's open door; and to-night she might listen specially. In the ordinary way he would have *had* to go down, if only to get his shoes; but he had come straight from the study to his own room without removing them, and though he had since put on a pair of slippers, the shoes were still there—luckily half concealed beneath the bed, so that Phemie had not noticed them. Neither had Mother, or she herself would have taken them away, as she had taken the tray; and it was most unlikely he would have any further visitor to-night.

Everything favoured his project. He had given no promise to Daddy, which was fortunate, for of course a prisoner on parole was bound by honour not to attempt to escape. He could climb down easily enough by the drain-pipe, and even if he fell part of the way it was no great height, and would be on to a flower-bed. Only he would have to wait till the house was perfectly quiet; and it wouldn't be safe to lie down on the outside of the bed, for he remembered his old plan of visiting the church at night, and how it had come to nothing because he had fallen asleep and slept till morning. . . .

Suddenly he heard the sound of Daddy's voice, and it appeared to be coming from immediately below his window. The dogs must be there too, and have been waiting patiently all this time, for Daddy was telling them to go home. Tom rushed to the window to look. Yes; both Roger and Barker were there; and he longed to make a signal but dared not. They were paying no attention to Daddy's orders, which rapidly became more peremptory, so that in the end Roger reluctantly began to move away. Barker, however, did not budge. He was lying at the edge of the lawn, and when Daddy, losing patience, pushed him with his foot, he growled. Tom couldn't actually hear the growl, but he could see it, and anyhow he could have told there was a growl from Daddy's immediate outburst of indignation. He even lifted a pebble from the drive and threw it at poor Barker. At this final insult Barker indeed got up, yet still he did not run away, but retired slowly and with dignity, leaving Daddy, Tom thought, looking both undignified and absurd.

It was another proof, if he had needed one, of the faithfulness of animal friendships, and in his present mood it not only consoled him but strengthened him in his determination. He would go. . . .

How long would it take him? He had never walked the whole

way to Granny's, and though of course he had often driven, it was very hard to judge of distances when you were in a car. It couldn't, he thought, be more than seven or eight miles—possibly less—and at any rate it didn't much matter when he arrived, since, at the soonest, Granny and everybody else would have been in bed for hours. . . .

It was too dark now to read and he dared not turn on the light. He would just have to sit in the darkness, doing nothing, till it was time for him to start.

CHAPTER XXIII

On that night of all nights it was just like Daddy to sit up later than usual, but at length Tom—who for the past hour had been dozing fitfully in his chair—now sleeping, now waking—heard him coming upstairs. The time for action was drawing nearer, and a strange thing was, that as it did so it became far more difficult to wait. He decided that if he drew down the blinds he might perhaps risk turning on the light, since sitting on tenterhooks like this made it impossible to gauge the passage of time, whereas, if he were to read say forty pages of Apollodorus or Frank Buckland, that would be practically as good as a clock, and by then, surely, Daddy would be asleep.

Doggedly—and taking in nothing of what he read—he went through with his task; after which he shut the book, put on his shoes, and carefully drew up the blind. He leaned far out over the sill, and the sweet fragrance of the stocks below his window rose to him through the night, friendly and reassuring. There was no moon, yet it was not really dark. He could make out the different constellations, shining clear and bright in the grey vault of the sky amid the twinkling of countless unknown stars, and through the pale glimmer they shed the trees rose black and solid, as through a milky sea. In this ashen half-light, so unlike the light of day, shrubs and bushes assumed fantastic shapes, and the trees seemed to stretch out beckoning arms, stirring softly in the wind, whispering with the whisper of innumerable leaves. Tom put one leg out of the window, and sitting astride the sill, leaned sidelong till he could reach the drain-pipe. This he grasped firmly before drawing out the other leg and clambering down. It was really quite easy, easier than he had expected, for the thick tough creeper gave plenty of support to his feet, and he accomplished the descent almost in silence.

The adventure had now begun, and once out on the road, with the gate closed behind him, his sense of it so entirely took possession of his mind that all else was forgotten. He was no longer running away; he was conscious only of freedom and of being at large in a strange nocturnal world he had never before explored.

He walked on steadily, soon leaving the more immediate and familiar surroundings behind him. The loneliness did not trouble him, though he would have liked Roger as a companion; but only for the sake of his company, not because he had any fears. He felt, in fact, both exhilarated and excited. A light breeze was blowing, but its coolness was merely pleasantly fresh, and it was behind him.

He must have walked two or three miles before a drop of rain fell. It was an uncommonly big drop, and it splashed on to his bare head so unexpectedly that he stopped and looked up in surprise. Somehow he had never thought of rain, yet now he saw that a black wall of cloud had overtaken him and as it advanced was extending rapidly on either side, eclipsing the stars and threatening soon to cover the whole sky. It would only be a shower, he hoped; indeed the large size of the raindrops and their warmth encouraged this view; but it would be a heavy plump while it lasted, and since there was what appeared to be a wood, or plantation, a little beyond the hedge on his left, he determined to seek shelter.

It was not really a wood, Tom found, on coming up to it; not much more than a thicket, composed for the greater part of laurels and rhododendrons; but crouching under these he was completely protected—at all events for the present and till they should be soaked through. Fortunately he had reached it in the nick of time, for the rain now came down in a torrent, like a thunder-shower without thunder, and heavy enough to have drenched him to the skin in a few minutes had he been out in the open. He wriggled in closer to the heart of the thicket, for the ground, though soft, was dry, and composed of a loose vegetable mould. Here he was snug enough, and the combination of the hour, the place, and the sound of the rain pattering on the broad leaves above him, created a sense of solitude such as he had never before known. It was as if, so far as human beings were concerned, he had the whole world to himself, and yet this feeling, though very strange, was by no means unpleasant. On the contrary, it was happy, it was dreamily peaceful, and mingled with it was also the feeling that another and lovely world was near—so near that a sign, a message, possibly a visitor from it, seemed on the point of breaking through. Crouching there, hidden in his leafy den, a hushed and expectant eagerness shone out through his eyes as clearly as a light shining through a window: he was himself, at that moment, half boy, half spirit. . . .

But the rain was nearly over; most of it at present was dropping from the bushes, not from the clouds; and like some small nocturnal animal, Tom crept forth from his shelter.

The cloud-bank had passed on, uncovering once more the starry vault above it, and there once more, far far away in the remoteness of space, were his old friends, the Great Bear, Orion with his belt, the chair of Cassiopeia.

Back on the road, he resumed his tramp, and kept it up for a long time with no noticeable slackening of pace, though he was beginning to feel tired, and sometimes sat down on a low wall or on a bank of stones to rest.

He must be a good many miles from home now. Gradually, too, the surrounding fields were becoming greyer and objects more distinct as the sky lightened. The stars were fading in the twilight of approaching dawn, and presently they disappeared altogether, and a crimson flush swept up above the eastern horizon. This was followed swiftly by a golden shaft of light, and then by the whole edge of the sun's flaming disk: the new day was here.

But Tom's journey was ended, for he had reached Granny's. He passed through the gate and up the avenue to the sleeping house amid the first twittering of drowsy birds. It would be still some hours, he knew, before the servants made an appearance, and there was nothing to be done in the meantime but sit down on the doorstep and wait. He was on the point of doing this, when he remembered that in the open yard at the back of the house there was a dog-kennel, and a very large one, though Granny had never possessed a dog, and the kennel dated back no doubt to ancient Seaford days. It had been specially built, too, for not only was it bigger than usual, but also—supported on four thick squat legs—it stood some inches above the ground and was covered with waterproof sheeting, while, apart from the customary dog's entrance, the entire front was made to slide backwards and forwards along grooves, so that it could be cleaned out more effectively. Of course it must be a long time since it *had* been cleaned out, and it was sure now to be dusty and cobwebby. But Tom wasn't afraid of dust and cobwebs, and if he curled himself up there would be at least sufficient if not plenty of room. The idea—bringing with it an immediate vision of Roger and Barker, both probably at this moment fast asleep in their kennels—appealed to him strongly. Three minutes later he had put it into execution.

CHAPTER XXIV

He had rolled up his jacket to make a pillow, and he was so tired that after a while, in spite of the hardness of a bare wooden floor and the discomfort of his narrow quarters, he fell asleep, though it was not a sound sleep, and the unbolting of the back door awoke him at once. Peeping out, he saw that it was Rose coming to get coals from the coalhole, and at any ordinary time he would have enjoyed giving her a start. Now, however, he did not feel much in the mood for playing tricks, and merely said softly: "I'm here, Rose."

Nevertheless, Rose uttered a half-stifled scream and dropped her shovel, though she still clung to the bucket. The scream brought Cook, and they both stood stock-still, side by side, gazing in mute astonishment at a rather sheepish Tom, who—feeling cold, stiff, and at a low ebb generally—emerged with some difficulty from his unusual bedchamber.

Cook recovered first, or at any rate first found words. "My sakes! In the name of goodness what's happened to you and where have you been? Just look at the state of him!" And they both looked, which really was not surprising, for you can't burrow in loose earth under laurel bushes, and sleep in disused dog-kennels, without accumulating a certain amount of grime, and Tom had accumulated more than he realized. His hands and knees were black, his face was streaked with dirt, and there were cobwebs in his hair. As for his clothes——! But Cook made a sudden grab at him, caught him by the shoulders, and hurried him on into the house without further speech.

A fire was roaring good-temperedly in the kitchen range, and he held out his hands to the genial blaze, seeing which, Cook drew forward a chair and plumped him into it. "What the mistress will say I don't know!" she began. "I'm going to make her morning tea now, for she likes it early, and it's gone seven."

She stood over him, as if uncertain what to do next, while Rose, who had returned with her coal-bucket, also hovered near. Both, Tom saw, having got over their first consternation, were now consumed with a burning curiosity, yet at the same time they seemed worried—Cook especially. "You look just about worn out," she commiserated, "which I'm sure is little wonder." Turning from him, she shook her head dubiously before proceeding to make tea in two pots—one for the present company, he supposed, and one for Granny.

"What am I to tell her?" the more lackadaisical Rose murmured, casting an uneasy glance at the tray Cook was preparing.

The question was not addressed to Tom, but it was he who

answered it. "You neeɑn't tell her anything," he said. "I'm going up myself, and I'll tell her."

This brought Cook round to him again for a further inspection. "You can't," she declared peremptorily. "Leastways, not till I've cleaned you up a bit first."

She had poured him out a cup of tea, which he drank, and then began munching biscuits from the tin. The tea revived him, and he drank a second cup; while all the time they watched him as if he were Edward or Alfred eating nuts or bread-and-milk. "I'll clean myself afterwards," he mumbled, with his mouth full of biscuit. "I'm going to speak to Granny first. What's the good of waiting—when she'll want to see me anyhow. . . . Besides, there's nothing to tell—except that I'm here, and arrived too early, and got into the kennel."

"You mean to say you've been walking all night—and by yourself—and all those miles!" Cook exclaimed, while Rose simultaneously put in a feeble "Well I never!"

But this wonder-struck attitude was beginning to pall on Tom, and he answered impatiently: "Of course I've been walking all night. How do you think I got here if I didn't walk . . . ? Sorry!" he added next moment, a little ashamed of his irritability; and when Rose lifted the tray to carry it upstairs, he followed her—though he lingered outside on the landing until he heard her announcing in awe-stricken tones, "Master Tom's here."

Granny was sitting up in bed, and he ran forward to kiss her before she had time to speak. She didn't behave like Rose and Cook, and he had known she wouldn't. Certainly she looked astonished, but she didn't gasp or stare or throw up her hands, nor did she seem to mind his being dirty. "I've run away, Granny," he whispered impetuously into her ear. "I had to, because Daddy wants me to say I'm sorry to Mr. Sabine and I won't. Max killed my squirrel, and I took his gun and threw it in the river, and——"

But Granny was saying "Ssh—ssh", and he stopped, while she spoke to Rose, who having deposited the tray on a table beside the bed, still lingered near the door. "See first of all that he gets a bath, Rose. You might prepare it now: I suppose the water's hot. . . .

"And after that you're to go straight to bed," she went on, turning to Tom. "You can tell me everything later; but not another word now. By the time you're undressed, Rose will have the bath ready, and the moment you come out of it you're to go to bed and to sleep till I call you. Rose will make up the bed while you're having your bath, and she can take away your things and clean them. . . . Be a good boy, now, and do as I tell you. We'll have plenty of time to talk afterwards, so meanwhile just show me how good you *can* be."

She smiled, gave him a pat on the hand and a friendly little push, and in return, determined to obey literally, Tom departed without one further syllable, going to the room he always slept in, while Rose went to the bath-room, where he heard her turning on the taps.

He undressed slowly, giving the bath plenty of time to fill. But it was very pleasant to get his soiled clothes off, and still pleasanter when, having made his way to the bath-room, he was lying soaking in the warm water. He allowed his limbs to relax deliciously. Stretched at full length, he lay quite still, with his eyes closed. All the same, it wouldn't do to fall asleep, which he began to feel might easily happen if he wasn't careful. . . .

Presently there was a knock on the door—Rose again—this time to tell him she had made his bed and was taking his clothes down to the kitchen to see what could be done with them. Rose must have recovered, for her voice sounded admonitory and slightly aggrieved. Later she would leave the clothes on a chair outside his door, she said, where he would find them when he got up. Tom thanked her drowsily, and getting out of the bath began to dry himself. This finished, he opened the door about two inches, just to make sure the coast was clear before scuttling across the landing to his bedroom.

There, the first thing he did was to look to see if Rose had stuck a hot jar in his bed, and of course she had. He removed it. As if anybody wanted hot jars—particularly in the middle of summer! But it was always the same at Granny's: she herself actually liked two! Raising the bedclothes, with a little sigh of satisfaction he slid naked between the sheets, and before he had quite decided what he was going to think about was wrapped in a slumber too deep for dreams.

It was Granny who awakened him. She did not come in, but merely tapped on the door, and when he answered told him lunch would be ready in a few minutes. Tom yawned and stretched himself luxuriously. He felt warm and extremely comfortable. All the tiredness and stiffness had passed out of his bones, and the boy who presently ran downstairs to Granny was very different from the weary and travel-stained one who had visited her a few hours earlier.

"Well, you look 'slept' at any rate," was the old lady's rather dry comment when he entered the room, feeling not only "slept" but quite recovered. She inspected him with an air of strict neutrality, as of one temporarily reserving judgement. "And now," she went on, when they were seated at the table, "you'd better give me *your* version of this escapade."

He did so, omitting nothing, nor had he only one listener, for during the progress of his story Rose found so many pretexts for lingering in the room that in the end Granny had to tell her, "That will do, Rose; I think we have everything we want."

So Rose had to clear out, though with such obvious reluctance that Tom thought it rather unkind of Granny. He understood her reason, all the same, when having waited till the door was closed, she said: "I've been talking to your mother on the telephone. I rang her up as soon as I could to tell her you were here, and fortunately I got her in time. . . . I mean, they hadn't yet missed you, as only the servants were down. Otherwise, I imagine, she would have been even more astonished and more upset than she was—which is saying a good deal. . . . Suppose, for some reason she had gone to your room in the middle of the night and found you weren't there! How could she possibly have known where you were or what had happened to you?"

"I'm sorry," Tom murmured repentantly. "I know I ought

to have left a note or something, and I would have if I'd remembered."

Granny herself knew he would; therefore all she answered was: "She told me she would be over in the afternoon, probably by teatime."

It was enough for Tom, however, who had not contemplated such rapid action. It altered indeed the entire prospect, and he turned two startled eyes on Granny's mild though at present distinctly non-committal countenance. "Then—Daddy will be coming too," he faltered.

"I don't think so," Granny replied.

"But he will," Tom persisted. "How can she come without him? She can't drive the car, and there's nobody else."

Granny guessed what he was thinking, and for a minute or two deliberately allowed him to go on thinking it before she said quietly: "I told her I should like to keep you for a few days, and in the end she agreed that this might perhaps be best—if she could persuade your father to consent to it. She said she would ask him, at any rate, though she very much feared he would insist on your coming home at once."

Tom listened with a clouded and brooding expression on his face. Past experience enabled him to picture the scene only too clearly—Mother's proposal, Daddy's reception of it, Mother's reply, and the ensuing arguments and discussion—much more suggestive of a conflict of wills than of "persuasion".

Granny noticed the worried look in his eyes, but mistook its origin. "She rang me up again—about two hours later—to tell me Doctor Macrory was going to drive her over, and that she would bring whatever things you required."

"That means Daddy's furious," Tom said darkly.

Some such suspicion had in fact crossed Granny's own mind—particularly since, in the later communication, her son-in-law's name had not been mentioned. So she replied: "Well, if he is, it ought to show you what comes of being self-willed and disobedient. Other people, who are perfectly innocent, have to suffer for it."

"But Granny; I told you exactly *everything* that happened, and *you* didn't seem so very angry!"

"That's not the same at all. In your father's position I dare say I should have been. And now he'll very likely feel offended too. . . . Which, in all the circumstances, I must say doesn't strike me as surprising."

Tom sat in silence, frowning. The silence was prolonged, for Granny, perhaps again on purpose, forbore to break it. At last he said: "Maybe I'd better go home."

To his surprise, this sudden and belated compliance had far from the anticipated effect. Granny, in fact, asked him quite sharply: "Do you mean by that you are now willing to apologize to Mr. Sabine?"

"No," Tom muttered.

"Then perhaps for once you'll allow other people to decide what is the best thing to do—and nothing can be decided until your mother comes."

CHAPTER XXV

Lunch over, Tom went out to talk to Quigley, who, whatever his shortcomings as a gardener, possessed one great advantage over William, in that he was a most sociable person. So they pottered about together, Tom following like a dog close on Quigley's heels, while they kept up a familiar if broken stream of conversation. Among other things, they discussed William himself; Quigley in a mock-serious vein, and illustrating his appreciation of that irreproachable person with several anecdotes, which if not strictly veracious, were at least new to Tom and amusing. Thus the time passed till they heard the sound of the approaching car.

Tom had left the gate open for it, and a few seconds later it swept up the drive, bringing not only Doctor Macrory and Mother, but also a most unexpected Pascoe, whom he had supposed to be still far away in Donegal. The usual bustle of alighting ensued—accompanied by greetings of various kinds—an embrace from Mother, a friendly "Hello!" from Pascoe, and a slap on the back from Doctor Macrory—in the midst of which Granny appeared at the top of the steps to welcome her visitors.

Mother looked worried, and as if she very much wished the others weren't there. But, backed up by Tom's verbal asseverations, an anxious inspection persuaded her that outwardly at least he was none the worse for his adventure, and just at present there was no opportunity for more. Pascoe had dragged out a suitcase, which Tom took from him, and they all moved together towards the house, with the exception of Doctor Macrory, who refused to come in, but promised to return later in time for tea and to take Mother home. With this assurance the doctor got back into his car, and they waited to see him start—Mother and Granny on the doorstep, the two boys close beside him on the drive; so that after leaning out to wave *au revoir* to the ladies he was able to catch Tom's eye, and by a wink convey a private message that all was well.

At least this was how Tom interpreted it, and he was about to follow Mother and Granny into the house when the latter suggested that he should leave down the suitcase for Rose to look after, adding that she and Mother wished to have a little chat together, and that in the meantime he might like to entertain his friend by showing him the garden and the grounds. . . .

Nothing loath, for Doctor Macrory's signal had had a most cheering effect, Tom deposited his burden. "Come on," he said gaily to Pascoe; and as soon as he got him alone: "When did you get back, and how did they manage to pick you up?"

"I got back yesterday," Pascoe replied sedately, "and I rode over to your house after lunch to-day. They were just starting when I arrived, so your mother told me where you were and asked me if I'd like to come with them."

"I suppose that means you'll have to go back with them," Tom reflected. "It's a pity you didn't ride over on your bike: then you could have stayed all evening. . . . I must say," he went on, "you didn't write many letters—considering all the fuss you made about getting *me* to write!"

Pascoe admitted the truth of this. "I meant to—honestly: but somehow or other I was always prevented—or else I was too sleepy—or——. Anyhow, we needn't bother about that now: tell me what's happened."

The expression on Tom's face, which prior to these words had betokened a remarkable revival in his spirits, immediately altered. All the troubles and difficulties, from which the arrival of the car and its occupants had temporarily distracted his thoughts, now came back with a rush, and he wondered how much Pascoe knew—if indeed he really knew anything and were not merely trying a shot in the dark? "Why?" he asked warily. "What makes you think something's happened?"

Pascoe shrugged his shoulders. "Because I know it has."

Tom looked at him, but gained no information from the calm gaze which met his own. "Did Mother say anything?" he questioned doubtfully.

"Not to me: I don't suppose she would before Doctor Macrory. All the same, I knew at once that something must be up."

"I don't see why," Tom muttered, far from pleased. Of course sooner or later he would have confided in Pascoe, but just at present he was sick of repeating the same story again and again, and this persistence made it inevitable. To get done with it as quickly as possible, he produced a bald and much abbreviated account, to which Pascoe listened without comment. Tom didn't care. In fact he was rather glad Pascoe said nothing—even if it meant that like everybody else he disapproved. For by now he felt so weary of the whole thing that all he wanted was to forget it. Perhaps it was this that brought back to memory an old plan, which recent events had thrust into the background of his mind. Certainly he could have no better opportunity than the present for putting it into practice, and it would at least save him from having to talk about Mr. Sabine and Max. Not that he himself felt in the right mood. Very definitely he didn't, but that couldn't be helped; and besides, it was what Pascoe would feel—

if he felt anything at all—that mattered. At all events he might as well try the experiment and see what happened. . . .

"Let's go in," he proposed, turning back towards the house.

Pascoe made no movement to follow him. "I don't think they want us," he said dubiously. "Your grandmother practically told us she didn't."

"Oh, Granny won't mind: why should she?" And since Pascoe, in spite of this assurance, still hung back: "I don't mean to *them* of course, if that's what you're thinking. I mean upstairs—to a part of the house Granny doesn't even use. It's been shut up ever since she came here."

But Pascoe, possibly failing to see how this constituted an attraction, continued to hesitate. It was obvious that he would very much prefer to explore the grounds outside, and that only his status as a visitor prevented him from saying so. "Oh, all right," he finally gave in, but with such a marked absence of enthusiasm that at any other time Tom would have abandoned the project. Now, however, Pascoe's unwillingness was ignored; he was led indoors; Tom got the key; and they ascended the stairs together to the disused wing.

Yet nothing was going right. Conscious of Pascoe's latent antagonism, Tom already felt discouraged, and it was with but the faintest echo of his former thrill of expectancy that he unlocked the door at the end of the passage. Pascoe, still hankering after the sunlight and the unexplored grounds outside, clearly felt no thrill whatever; nor, as he rather sulkily followed his conductor, did he try to conceal his dissatisfaction at being dragged upstairs—apparently to gaze at three or four abandoned rooms, with nothing in them except some more or less dilapidated furniture and a few mouldy old books. Pascoe very obviously was bored, and notwithstanding all efforts to the contrary, his unresponsiveness and complete lack of interest were producing a more and more damping effect upon Tom himself. There, in the window, was the table, with the pile of *Graphics* still open upon it; outwardly, in spite of all the dusting and scrubbing, little was changed since he had been here last; yet in an inner and spiritual sense everything was changed. The beauty and the wonder and the sense of haunting were gone; he even began to see it all as Pascoe saw it—an abandoned room, some more or less dilapidated furniture, and a few mouldy old books. He turned, and a question hovered on his lips, but died unspoken as Pascoe asked bluntly; "Is this *all*?"

The accentuation of the final word completed what had been nearly accomplished without it. "Yes," Tom answered. "We'll go down."

His abrupt and unexpected acquiescence—perhaps because it *was* unexpected—seemed to produce more effect than his earlier eagerness, for it was with a quite genuine curiosity that Pascoe now glanced at him. "Why were you so anxious to bring me up, then?" he said. "You *were*, you know, though now you seem to have changed your mind."

Tom turned away. "I thought you might like it," he replied.

"Like what? What is there *to* like? I don't believe you thought any such thing. You had a particular reason, and now, as usual, you're making a mystery about it."

"Well, I haven't any longer," Tom said, "so it doesn't matter. . . . There's the gong," he continued with relief, as the sound came up to them, faint and muffled, from the hall below. "Doctor Macrory must have come back, so we'd better go down."

The interruption was welcome. His proposed experiment had faded out so flatly that it could not even be said to have ended, since it had never begun. Or rather, what had faded out was his own enthusiasm, his own responsiveness. His present reaction almost amounted to a feeling of disillusionment, and as they retraced their steps along the passage, and he locked the door behind them, he half made up his mind never to open it again.

To come downstairs was to come at once into a comfortable prosaic world where, if nothing was particularly enthralling, all was safe and familiar. Mother, Doctor Macrory, and Granny had already begun tea when he and Pascoe entered, Granny presiding at the table. The sunshine streaming through the open windows made the room attractively gay, but it was gay also with that general atmosphere of cheerfulness and geniality which this most informal and conversational of meals seems particularly to promote. Moreover, whether by previous arrangement or not, evidently it had been decided to regard Tom's visit to Granny, not as the result of home complications, but as a perfectly ordinary one. Granny herself made this doubly clear, when, after urging Pascoe to try Cook's slimcakes, she invited him to stay for a day or two to keep Tom company.

For some private reason this appeared to amuse Doctor Macrory. "What about the Dogs' Club?" he suggested. "That is, if you want to do the thing really in style. I think I can accept so far as Barker is concerned."

It was a very transparent joke; nevertheless Mother, knowing both Tom and Granny, thought it prudent to intervene. "I fancy if she has two gentlemen to look after her that will be sufficient."

Tom and Doctor Macrory laughed, but Granny had never heard of the Dogs' Club, and Pascoe saw nothing to laugh at. Granny had turned again to him, this time to inquire if they had a telephone at home. "If so, you could ring your mother up after tea. That is, if you think you'd like to stay."

Pascoe thought he would like it very much, but on the other hand, supposing he got his mother and she gave him permission, wouldn't he still have to go home first to get pyjamas and other necessaries; and he had left his bicycle at Tom's house.

"I'm sure Tom can lend you all you need for to-night," Granny declared. "And you can get anything else to-morrow."

Doctor Macrory, with his customary good nature, endorsed this view. "His best plan will be to come with us now in the car. I'll have to be going in a few minutes anyhow. Afterwards he can ride back here on his bicycle, and I dare say you'll forgive him if he's a little late for dinner."

Mother alone, for a moment looked doubtful: but seeing Pascoe getting up to put Granny's suggestion into execution, she left her misgivings unspoken, and after a brief hesitation said: "In the meantime, while Clement is telephoning, I think Tom and I will take a stroll in the garden. You'll find us there when you're ready to start."

She rose from her chair as she spoke, and Tom followed her,

not surprised, for he had known she would want to speak to him by himself before leaving, but wondering a little what she was going to tell him.

She began at once. "I saw Miss Sabine this morning: in fact I had a long talk with her. I don't know whether you realize what a good friend you have in Miss Sabine. Nobody could have been kinder or nicer about this whole unfortunate business than she was, and I think you might do something in return—something to please her, to please Daddy, and to please me."

Tom desired nothing more than to please Miss Sabine and to please Mother; about Daddy he felt less keen. "What do you want me to do?" he asked.

"To write a little note to Mr. Sabine; that is all."

Tom hesitated, his face clouding. Mother might pretend it wasn't much, but she must know it meant abandoning his whole position, and admitting he was wrong when he wasn't. "To tell him I'm sorry?" he muttered unwillingly.

"Yes. Remember this is entirely between ourselves: I purposely said nothing to Daddy about it in case you might refuse."

He waited a moment, Mother's hand on his shoulder. He felt that by putting the matter in this way she was somehow imposing on him, but he knew she would be deeply hurt if he were to tell her so. All the same, he could not help looking at her reproachfully before, with a faint sigh, he submitted. "All right," he said. "But I won't really be sorry—I mean in the way he'll think—not about him and Max."

Mother did not press this point: she drew a breath of relief. "I'm sure if you write the note and show it to Granny before sending it, you will be doing what is right, and will never regret it afterwards."

Tom was very far from sure, but since he would be doing it to please Mother and Miss Sabine, not Mr. Sabine or Max, and since he could make the note extremely cold and formal—in fact thoroughly unconvincing—he promised; nor was there time for much more before the others appeared, and Mother, Doctor Macrory, and Pascoe got into the car.

Tom and Granny saw them off, standing side by side; and

when the car had disappeared and they had re-entered the house, he told Granny of his promise. She, too, seemed relieved, and between them, and with many consultations and fresh starts, they proceeded to compose the momentous letter, not without some chuckles from the old lady, though Tom could see nothing funny in his efforts to keep his word to Mother and at the same time not to encourage Mr. Sabine to imagine he had really changed his mind or regarded him with anything but the most frigid and distant politeness. The task was difficult, but Granny, entering into the spirit of it, was very helpful; and the rough draft at last completed, he copied it out, addressed the envelope, and left it on the hall table for the postman to collect.

CHAPTER XXVI

Granny was much surprised when after dinner her guests, instead of going out to the garden as she had expected them to do, suggested playing a game of Pelmanism, or, as they called it, Twos. Still, if that was what they wanted she was quite agreeable, and anyhow, after last night's performance, she had decided to send Tom to bed early. Granny, however, entirely mistook the situation, and this because she knew nothing of a private consultation in which the question of her own entertainment had been very carefully weighed. It never crossed her mind that the game of Twos might have been proposed for her benefit, nor did it subsequently strike her that, with her rather dim old eyes and their remarkably bright ones, it was, to say the least, surprising that she should win. Nevertheless, win she did; and the game over, and the card-table put away, good-nights were said—with final injunctions from Granny that there was to be no dawdling, and no talking after they were in bed.

But such instructions are received as a matter of course, as part of a conventional formula, and enter in at one ear straightway to go out at the other. Once in bed, Pascoe had a number of things to relate about his visit to Aunt Rhoda in Donegal, and from these, by easy transitions, the conversation drifted, first to their present visit, and next to Tom's previous visits at Tramore. Following on the activities of a very crowded day, the darkness and stillness and sense of comfort and privacy induced a mood of confidence, and without being questioned, without indeed remembering his earlier uncommunicativeness, Tom found himself telling Pascoe why he had taken him up to the deserted wing, and what had happened there on a former occasion. The story came at first fluently, but, as it proceeded, more and more brokenly and with increasingly longer pauses, though Pascoe continued to listen attentively—so attentively that he made neither a movement nor a sound to interrupt it. Even after it was finished the silence still persisted, and it was only then that Tom, growing suspicious, discovered him to be sound asleep.

He was not offended; he had been talking really, towards the end, as much to himself as to his companion; and now he felt too drowsy to wonder at what point Pascoe had ceased to hear him. That, he would learn to-morrow, and in the meantime he was content to lie in dreamy contemplation of a world shifting uncertainly between recollection and imagination. Nor was he surprised to see, amid drifting scenes and faces, Ralph himself standing between the window and the bed. By that time, too, he must have forgotten Pascoe, or surely he would have awakened him, whereas all he did was to murmur sleepily; "Why have you come?"

The voice that answered him was faint and thin as the whisper of dry corn. "I don't know. I don't think I have come. I don't think this is real. . . . Or perhaps I can only come when you are dreaming, for I think you are dreaming now. . . ."

There was a silence—deep, wonderful, unbroken—as if all the restless murmuring whispers of earth and night were suddenly stilled. . . .

"Listen!"

Tom listened, but somehow Ralph was no longer there; and far, far away he could hear the sound of waves breaking, and surely he had heard that low distant plash before—many times perhaps, though when and where he had forgotten. Next moment the darkness vanished, and he had a vision of a wide, curving beach of yellow sand, where children were playing in the sunlight at the edge of a timeless sea. They were building castles on the sand, and their happy voices reached him—gay, innocent, laughing. Vision or memory, the scene brought with it no feeling of strangeness, only the sense of returning to a lovely and familiar place, which would always be there, though at times it might be hidden from him. . . .

The dark blue water stretched out and out under a golden haze, till it met the softer, paler blue of the sky. That happy shore he knew—and it was drawing closer, it seemed very near, already less dream than reality. For he could feel the warm sun on his hands and face, and he had to step back quickly as a small wave curled over and broke, melting and hissing, in a thin line of foam at his feet. . . .

November 1942.
October 1943.